# Tя aumata

## The Seasons of Femininity

Publisher: www.sakurabookpublishing.com
alta@sakurabookpublishing.com


ISBN: 978-1-0370-7786-9(print)

978-1-0370-7787-6(e-book)

## MORE BY THE AUTHOR

### Poetry

*To All the Vultures*
The Paper Trail Literary Journal

*Three in One*
South African Verses Anthology

*Earth, Our Mother, Our Child*
Poetry is Not Dead Anthology

### Short Story

*Nothing but Lights*
320 Days of Sunshine Anthology

*This book is dedicated to my mother and little brother,*
*Yasmeen and Kaycé.*
*With whom I have shared my trauma.*

# FOREWORD

"Traumata – The Seasons of Femininity" by Sonia Naidoo is a profoundly moving and poetic exploration of trauma, identity, and healing through the lens of femininity.

Naidoo's lyrical and detailed writing offers readers an intimate glimpse into her experiences and emotions. The narrative skillfully intertwines introspection with evocative imagery, creating a haunting yet resonant story that lingers long after the final page has been read.

The book's prose is exquisite, with passages like "Red is a writer who chronicled her suffering, and I'm just the reader of her sorrows," which captures the tension and suspense that keep readers engaged. Naidoo's ability to blend poetic language with storytelling makes this work a masterful example of literary art.

"Traumata – The Seasons of Femininity" is highly recommended for those seeking a thought-provoking and emotionally rich read. It is a testament to the power of storytelling in exploring complex themes of identity, belonging, and trauma. This book is sure to leave a lasting impression on its readers.

**James N. McManus** — Author of Travels a Poetic Journey and Poetry from Afar.

*'You shall not dwell in tombs made by the dead for the living.*
*And though of magnificence and splendour, your house shall*
*not hold your secret nor shelter your longing.*
*For that which is boundless in you abides in the mansion of*
*the sky, whose door is the morning mist, and whose windows*
*are the songs and the silences of night.'*

—Kahlil Gibran, *The Prophet*

# SHEKINAH

## *Revelations*

"Is this house a home? And if not, then what is a home?"

"I can tell you what it's not. It's not the peeling paint on the walls or the carefully chosen décor that your parents cherished. Nor the little trinkets they hoarded and scattered throughout their mortal dwelling. It's not the aroma of your mother's cooking after a sweltering day at school or the way familiar laundry fluttered in the wind. It's not the water-stained ceilings of your father's dilapidated, cursed house. It's not even your family that resides within its confines.

"A home is not a physical structure. It's a sense of belonging. Home is divine intervention, a psychoanalysis close to catharsis, and an emotion just shy of agape love. To say one feels like home is to make oneself vulnerable. Man is born with an insatiable yearning to belong to a tribe, a nation, a government, a country, a home, and a God. Abide in me, and I will abide in you."

"But what happens if I don't belong anywhere?"

"Trauma takes root."

"Why?"

"Because the human soul was never designed to wander in solitude."

"Where does trauma take root?"

"In the way your mother plaits your hair, in the thunder of your father's voice, in your brother's silent tears, in the house of shadows you once called home, and in your name. Deep within hidden crevices, the roots cling, its presence veiled until time ripens the bitter fruits of trauma. This is a war only you can declare an end to."

"A war between me and who?"

"You and death."

# ED

## 24th February 2012

*I'm not sure why my father named me Red.*

My mother wished to name me Josephine, while my Nana insisted that Sadiya was a name better suited to me. Josephine reminded my mum of her favourite biblical tale of Joseph and his coat of many colours. My Nana, however, saw Sadiya as a name that evoked the luck and fortune he believed I brought into the world at my birth. Both names carried the weight of hope for them, yet neither seemed to belong to me. It all came to nought, for, in the end, my father prevailed.

Red, on the other hand, screamed danger. Buttons of disasters were painted red, and red doors warned us never to enter.

*Why did he name me Red?* I recalled the origin of my name and how my father claimed he chose it.

One summer day, he decided to venture into town. He stood patiently at the bus stop, and when the bus arrived, he quietly took a seat at the back, far away from the white passengers. After a brief ride into the city, he continued his journey on foot and headed towards the cinema.

He often reminisced about how, for just R25, one could purchase a bag of popcorn, a cold drink and a movie ticket. I recalled how he would often pause to marvel at such prices, and my mum would do the same every time they shared a story with me about their past.

*I'm not complaining.*

It was truly fascinating to hear tales of bubble gum costing just a single cent, and all the smallest of things mattered back then. Yet, on this particular trip to the cinema, my father went to watch a specific film. A Russian war movie. In this haunting narrative, civilians perished under Russia's arsenal. Women, children, the elderly, both the innocent and guilty, died. At the heart of the story loomed a formidable submarine, a behemoth of destruction, ominously named Red.

*What did my dad think when he named me Red?* I felt as though my name never suited my face.

I pictured my father sitting in the vintage cinema, eyes fixed on the waterborne killing machine as it flickered on the big screen. He observed its cold, menacing presence, a million useless buttons on the control panel, and lifeless metal everywhere. Monotony suffocated its interior. Weapons and warfare! These were the things that drew affection from my father. He watched the cinematic submarine and immediately thought of something.

He thought of me.

*Red.*

The hue of roses, dead or alive. A prostitute's painted lips. A woman's dress on her first date. Strawberries in a white bowl. Cherry ice-lollies on a sunny day. The title of a tongue twister.

*Red.*

Ladybugs on careful fingertips. A teenager's first period. The tape around dead bodies. The hair colour of a heartbroken woman. The blush of new lovers. Painted nails on an Autumn Day. A Russian submarine.

*Red.*

The colour of the warm, metallic blood that dripped down my skinny arms as my room dissolved into darkness.

*'To be wounded by your understanding of love;*
*And to bleed willingly and joyfully.'*

—Kahlil Gibran, *The Prophet*

# SHEKINAH

## *26th March 2012*

"Dad, her case seems too serious." I stared nervously at the medical file in my hands. "What if I mess this up?" The patient was only 16 years old, and she had previously been seeing a therapist who clearly couldn't help her.

"Fucking government hospitals."

"That's Doctor to you, missy, and what's with the cussing?" Dad finally responded from his desk. His gruff voice cut through my spiralling thoughts.

*Did I say that out loud?*

"Now is not the time to be sarcastic." I walked briskly to him and slammed the file down on his shiny oak desk. "This child tried to commit suicide. How am I going to help her?" I choked up as the fear of failure snaked into my mind.

"Shekinah, you are qualified now. This is your job." He glanced at the file and continued, "As a professional and not as my daughter, I need you to show me your true potential. As it is, everyone thinks you're operating at this office because of nepotism. Prove them wrong. This is your passion because you want to help people. Now, someone needs your help, and you're too scared?"

A heavy silence fell upon us. I felt like a child again, waiting for Daddy's approval. I hated to admit it, but he was right. As doubt filled my mind, there was a soft knock at the office door, which we both chose to ignore. Dad slid the patient's file back to me and smiled gently.

"I read her file already, and I know you'll save this girl's life. I wouldn't have recommended you to her mother without being sure about it."

I felt a little hopeful and took the file from his hand. "Thanks... Doctor."

We grinned comically at each other as another soft knock resounded at the door.

"Come in!" He shouted, and the door opened slowly. Our receptionist poked her head through the gap.

"Patient named Red is here to see Dr. Shekinah," she chimed.

"Thanks. I'll be with her shortly." I smiled warmly until she disappeared behind the door.

"You got this, kiddo." Dad got up slowly from his swivelling chair and gave me a soft pat on the back.

"Thanks, Dad." I sighed deeply, fixed my coat and walked out of the comfort of my father's office.

The silence was deafening as I watched Red tug anxiously at her sleeves. Her eyes were vacant, and I could tell she had already slipped into a dark place.

"Why don't you tell me a little about yourself, Red?" I prayed my smile didn't appear as tense as I felt. She glanced at me through her lashes but quickly looked away. I knew she would be hard to reach, but I had to be patient.

Minutes ticked by in silence. I gently prodded her with

questions, and she responded with a curt nod or a subtle lift of her tiny shoulders. As she shrugged, her sleeve rolled up slightly, revealing the scars on her arms. Red noticed and quickly tugged at her sleeves, pulling them so tightly that I feared the fabric might tear.

"Can you tell me what happened there?" I motioned towards her wrists.

She began to pull on the loose threads of her clothes, her lowered eyes darted from left to right, and her anxiety visibly increased. I sensed a panic attack and quickly grabbed my rescue teddy from my desk.

"This is what I use to feel better." I extended the teddy to her, but she eyed it suspiciously.

"It's okay," I reassured her. "You don't have to talk until you're comfortable with me. Just hold the teddy for now."

After a moment's hesitation, she took the stuffed toy and pressed it tightly to her chest. Her breathing slowed as she focused on holding it close.

"It's okay to feel, Red," I continued softly. "Whether it's everything, all at once, or nothing at all. What's not okay is imprisoning those feelings." She glanced at me. Her grip on the teddy bear tightened and loosened in a rhythm of her own. I leaned forward slightly.

"It's okay if you don't want to speak, too, but you must allow yourself to feel. Bottling up your emotions will only make things worse. They'll become like prisoners in a cramped cell, and one day, those prisoners will find a way to break free." Her eyes softened, just a touch, and I took it as a small victory. "Do you know what happens to prisoners who try to escape?"

She shook her head.

"They get punished even more when caught, but that doesn't happen if they're released for good behaviour. It's the same with your feelings. When you let yourself feel your sadness, happiness, anger, and everything else, you can finally let go on the grounds of good behaviour. But if you keep everything imprisoned inside of you, it'll eventually break out in unhealthy ways." Red's eyes widened in realisation.

I glanced at her wrist, then at the clock on the wall behind her, surprised that our time was nearly up. Just as I was about to mention it, she broke the silence.

"I have a journal," she whispered.

I suppressed my excitement at her first words and asked, "Would you like to read it to me?"

She shook her head.

"That's fine," I encouraged her. "A journal is a perfect outlet for your feelings. Both the good and bad feelings. Every time you write what you feel, you face the realities within you, and that is very brave, Red."

She looked up at the mention of her name, and I saw a faint glimmer of hope in her eyes. Suddenly, the timer on my table rang. As I turned it off, she shot off the couch, grabbed her backpack, and stepped towards the door. She was halfway to her escape when she abruptly stopped. I observed as her back muscles tensed.

"Red, are you okay?" I asked.

She placed her backpack onto the floor and crouched to open the zipper. Her hand disappeared and emerged from the blackness with a small, pink journal. I said nothing as she approached me timidly and placed the journal before me.

"You can read it." Her voice was so hushed that I almost

13

didn't hear her. I picked up the book gently as if it were fragile.

"I will if that's really what you want."

"Yes." She nodded and pivoted on her heels. Her head was down, and her shoulders slumped as she walked out of the office and out of my sight.

### *27th March 2012*

The morning breeze cooled my skin as I sat on my front porch that overlooked the beach. Sea-shelled wind chimes tinkled softly above the side table, where Red's journal and a steaming cup of coffee lay in wait. I was sceptical about reading it at home as I had a rule against bringing work home, but Red's expectant eyes haunted me.

*I would read anything to help her.* The thought was as silent as Red's voice, but it empowered my body to move towards the journal.

I lifted it delicately and sauntered back to my rocking chair. I hadn't noticed the glitter on the cover until a ray of sunlight touched it. Hope filled me as I opened it and found doodles and then a quote. It looked like any other ordinary teenage girl's diary until I turned the page.

Written in bold on the stark white sheet was the name of a season, an ambiguous subtitle, and a drawing that sent chills down my spine. I paused, took a deep breath and dived into Red's journal.

*'For what is it to die but to stand naked in the wind and to melt into the sun?'*

—Kahlil Gibran, *The Prophet*

# SUMMER

*The Season of Innocence*

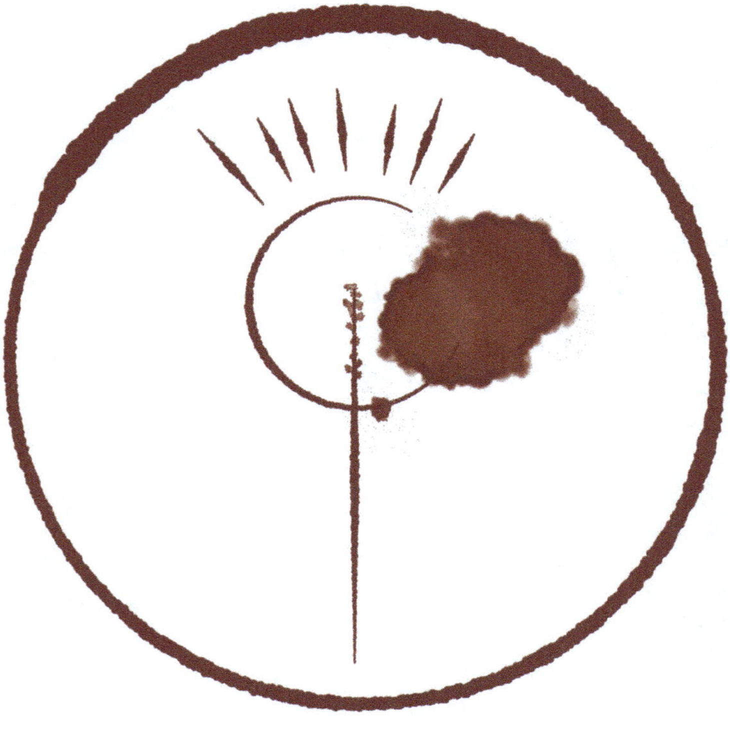

# THE MORAL OF THE STORY

"It's bedtime," Mama said with a mischievous grin.

I grinned back at her from the couch, kissed my Daddy goodnight, and ran at full speed on my little feet. When I reached Mama's room, I sprang onto the centre of the oversized bed and impatiently waited for her comforting presence. This was the best time of my day, when Mama read to me. She calmly walked towards me and then stopped at the edge of the bed. The book of the day was hidden behind her back, and I tried to guess which story it was.

*Is it the Christian pop-up book? It cannot be one of the big fairy-tale books because I don't see it peek-a-booing behind her. Maybe it's the tiny Little Mermaid fairy tale book. I love that one!*

I was bursting with excitement from guessing which book was hidden behind her tiny back. She smirked and slowly, *oh so very slowly*, revealed our story for the night.

"No way!" I exclaimed and clapped ecstatically, "Are you going to talk like him, Mummy? Are you going to talk like Gopher? And Eeyore? And Rabbit? And Roo?"

She laughed, sat on the bed, and calmed me down with a kiss on my bobbing head, "Of course, Sweetie. Is there any other way to read Winnie the Pooh?"

"Nah, uh, there isn't, and only you know how to read it and speak just like them!" I kicked under the covers and prepared myself for the most incredible story of them all. *Winnie the Pooh* was my ultimate favourite storybook.

*I mean, who doesn't love Pooh Bear? He's cute, chubby, and funny. He loves to eat honey, loves all his friends, and it's just the funniest thing ever when he gets stuck everywhere!*

I giggled at the memory of the last Pooh Bear story.

"Now," Mama interrupted my giggling, "remember to find the moral of the story."

She always said this before reading, but I didn't really know who or what a moral is. Mama said it's in every book I read, and I should always look out for it. She also said that people who read have a great imagination, which is rare. I didn't know the meaning of these strange words, but I couldn't wait to have an imagination and be rare. Mama began reading, and I listened intently to her, remembering to search for the moral of the story.

*Wow*, I thought as I stared at Mummy's face in amazement.

She spoke just like Pooh Bear, Roo, Rabbit and even my least favourite, Eeyore. She whistled through her teeth like Gopher, which always surprised me and left me rolling in laughter. She was magical. As she spoke in many different accents, her face seemed to change to match each one. Her hands moved up and down, left to right, and that simple action brought my favourite book to life.

She could change into a million different characters: a happy kangaroo, a sad donkey, a hungry bear, and a stuck-up rabbit. She could speak in a high and a low voice. She danced and sang, clapped and cried. My mummy changed who she was to make me smile.

I never knew that right at that moment, I found the moral of Mama's story.

# THE TISSUE-BOX BABY

Crying out in agony,
Only seven months pregnant,
Driven off in a car with Daddy.
Mummy was taken,
And all I remembered was
Nani's whole house was shaken.

Two weeks went by,
Mummy did not return.

"It doesn't look good."
"There are too many complications."
Cars drove up and down with the news.
I heard them say,
"We might need to take her bedroom shoes."

Four weeks went by,
Daddy came home.

"When do you think Mummy will come?"
"Today!" I say with childish joy.
He laughed and hugged me,
But later that night,
He did not bring my mummy.

Six weeks went by,
An announcement was made.

The family gathered around.
"I have a son!"
Daddy exclaimed proudly.
He failed to mention
That the baby was tissue-box-tiny.

Seven weeks went by,
We can finally visit Mummy.

The drive to the hospital was long,
The walk to Mummy, longer.
There she lay on the bed in slumber.
The pictures recall
A sweet day of love and wonder.

Eight weeks went by,
Mummy came home.

She laid the tiny baby on the plastic sofa covers,
As everyone surrounded him,
Speaking in languages only babies utter.
But Mummy fixed her eyes on me and said,
"Look after him, for this is your baby brother."

# ALF-A-SISTER

Her skin milky, and hair glossy,
Daddy's first little daughter.
Her beauty was praised by my father's family,
Wearing expensive clothes with pride and honour.

Gold jewellery adorned her from our Thatha,
Whilst R5 coins were tossed to me by my step-grandmother.
They secretly vowed never to accept us.
They loved her more than me and my brother.

Secret admirers gathered in her presence,
Popular in school with many crushes.
She taught me the word slut in grade seven,
It was the day I picked up my first paintbrushes.

Not understanding her whereabouts,
She packed her bags and moved around.
The morbid vision of my half-sister,
In my tears, forever drowned.

# SADIYA

In a little home, in Old Phoenix,
My mother's poor father lived.
On the day of my birth,
Unseen riches fell at his doorstep.
He held my tiny hand and wished a name upon me:
*Sadiya. My luck and fortune.*
A whispered dream.
A Muslim name,
That was never meant to be.

# OUR LITTLE APARTMENT

Blue and white,
The colours of happiness,
The colours of betrayal.
We stand on the balcony,
Taking one last look over the rail.

Daddy's best friend stole his business,
The man with the glasses,
The man with a villain's name.
He chased us from our shelter.
He thought he won the game.

But a miracle bloomed.
The night before the move.
"The house will be available in 24 hours"
Dad's new Mercedes was packed to the roof,
And our little apartment was never ours.

# THE HOUSE ON THE DEAD-END ROAD

The building loomed over us like a monster emerging out of a swamp. I shivered involuntarily as I stared up at it. The enormous wooden-framed front door gaped like a roaring mouth, its frame covered in vines and rotted from the salty air. Daddy always says that the ocean breeze kills everything within its reach, even if it's a few miles away. My parents were silent as they navigated the wild garden.

"We have a pool!" My brother screamed as he ran around the green, murky pool. Weeds grew from the surrounding sand, and frogs hopped everywhere like a plague.

*Ew.* I shivered again.

"You know what that means? If there's frogs, there's snakes!" Daddy said to us from somewhere in the bushes.

*Snakes? Can this place get scarier?* I wanted to cry, but held back my tears. I missed our little flat that was just a few roads away. It was small and neat, and the Olympic-sized pool was always clean. I heard a rustling in the trees behind me, and Daddy jumped out and grabbed me.

"Stop!" I squealed in between my bursts of hysterical laughter. He always forced a smile on us with a tickling battle. After what felt like forever, he finally stopped and placed me gently on the ground.

"Don't worry, it looks bad now, but give me some time. I will fix it up, and then you and your brother can swim every day."

I watched Daddy as he stared at the pool area. I could almost see his vision come to life in his sparkling eyes. I felt hopeful then. I had nothing to worry about because my dad was here, and he could fix anything.

"Let's go choose your room!" He beamed down at me, and I grinned back.

"I want this room!" I yelled excitedly. The small room was lit by the sun's rays that broke through the wooden-framed windows. I stood in the light, closed my eyes, and breathed deeply.

*Yes, this is my room!* I imagined myself curled up in a cosy corner, immersed in a book, while the sunlight burned my back. Daddy laughed as he listened to me rant about my plans to change it into a library.

"Remember, Red. You have to share your room with your little brother."

I pouted at this news and crossed my arms. "That's unfair!"

He raised his eyebrow at me, and I immediately uncrossed my arms and apologised.

"What did your mum teach you about sharing?"

"Sharing is caring. Sorry, Dad." He approved with a nod and walked out. I let out a long breath of air that I didn't know I was holding in.

*How am I going to share a room with Baxter? He pulls the blanket, and he pees in the bed!* As these thoughts played in my mind, my brother sprinted into the room with a toy car in each hand.

"Woah! I want a TV in here! Over there!" he screamed and pointed with a mischievous look. "We can watch cartoons the whole day!"

He held his toy car over his head and vanished from the room, making aeroplane noises. I stood alone, and all my anger towards my brother began to disappear.

He considered sharing with me without even a second thought. I felt terrible and secretly promised to always share with him, no matter what.

"Red! We're going out to eat now. What are you feeling for?"

"Whatever Baxter is feeling for!" I felt a sense of pride when I said that.

"I want Mcd's!" Baxter screeched from somewhere in the new house. His squeaky voice echoed everywhere and frightened me.

I ran out of the room and found Daddy and Baxter in the musty lounge. The wooden floors made a satisfying creak with every step I took. Daddy suddenly picked up Baxter and began a tickle battle with him. He giggled, wiggled his tiny body and tried to escape, but soon surrendered.

"I give up! I give up!" he begged as he cackled like a mad child. I shook my head and smiled at their antics, but I felt like something was missing.

*Where is Mama?* I turned to look for her, and there she was, standing in the kitchen and staring out the window. Like she used to do back at our flat, but on the balcony. I wondered then, and I wondered now, what she was thinking about. Or was she just admiring the jungle-like garden outside? I kind of liked the garden, too, and couldn't wait to read in it.

*So many reading spots!*

"I'm gonna get Baxter changed and ready," Dad interrupted my thoughts. I followed his gaze to where Mum stood, but she continued to stare out the window. I was worried that she had never heard him.

"Mhm," she finally mumbled after a few minutes of silence. I looked back at Dad, unsure of why I felt afraid.

He glared at her for a while, his nostrils flared, and his brows furrowed as Baxter grew restless in his arms. I felt like I was holding my breath again, but this time, my chest tightened, and I didn't understand why it began to burn like every Wednesday after swimming lessons. Eventually, Daddy sighed and strolled into the big bedroom on the far side of the house. The further he moved from Mama, the more the choking sensation in my throat subsided.

I walked into the kitchen and looked up at her. The blue around her eye was slowly fading away into an unpleasant green. Every time we went out, she covered it with makeup so the strangers wouldn't notice.

*I sometimes wish someone would notice.*

Her eyes looked glossy. It must have been from staring too long at the bright scenery outside.

I grabbed her hand and whispered, "Mama, do you like the new house?" She blinked, and a tear fell down her face. Slowly. It was as if time had frozen.

"If you and your brother love it, then so do I," she said.

ASTER

*Daddy wasn't always so bad.*

We used to have tickle battles and play catch in the flat, and Daddy got us every toy we liked. We had many fond memories with him. It was only when we moved into the big, scary house that the tickle battles slowly came to an end, and Mama cried more.

I remembered Daddy hitting her before we moved, but there was something about the house that made the beatings more memorable. I was very confused as to why Mama got *disciplined*. A big lady like her. Maybe it was normal for a husband to hit his wife, and maybe Mama was naughty, but it didn't feel right, and I was scared to tell Daddy that because I didn't want to get a hiding, too. Although he never hit us, we still lived in fear every day for Mama.

Baxter and I were excited to celebrate another Easter holiday in the big house, which looked less scary now because Daddy fixed it up. The only frightening thing was his anger towards Mama.

*I hope this Easter holiday will be fun, without any fights.*

As Daddy went to work, Mama prepared the house for the Easter weekend.

*I wonder where she'll hide the eggs this time.*

For the last couple of years, we have had the best Easter egg treasure hunts in our huge garden and all the rooms in our house. Mama gave us little baskets and Baxter and I competed to find the most eggs. I saw my little brother sneaking behind Mama all day, trying to figure out where she hid the eggs so he could beat me at the treasure hunt.

I chuckled as Baxter acted like a spy, hiding behind shadows and searching for clues. Mama was too busy in the kitchen to notice him climbing the wall and looking at the shelves for eggs. I knew she hadn't hidden them yet, but I left my brother searching for nothing. When the day ended and the sun began to set over the golf course, I noticed that Mama was upset. Tears pooled in her eyes, and I went to sit with her. I glanced at her phone and saw she was trying to call Daddy.

*Did something happen to him?* I wanted to ask, but I learned that children were not allowed to ask questions in an adult situation.

*And this feels like an adult situation.*

The sun disappeared, and the moon took its place as we waited for Daddy's return. However, the massive mechanical gate made no sound, and the phone calls were unanswered. Baxter began to feel uneasy too as he slowly realised that Daddy wasn't home, yet.

*Where is he? Is he okay? Who will protect us? Who will play with us now? Who will I watch National Geographic with now?*

"Is Daddy coming for the Easter egg hunt?" Baxter asked Mama, and her sullen eyes filled with tears again.

"No, Baxter. I don't think so."

That night, we went to bed hopeful that in the morning, Daddy would return with an adventurous story about why he had gone missing. But the Easter weekend went by in a haze, and he never returned. No eggs were found either. Mama took Daddy's special drinks from the cupboard and left them on the kitchen counter.

*Daddy and his friends must be coming,* I thought expectantly.

But every day, Mama poured glass after glass for herself and went into a deep sleep while Baxter and I wandered around the house searching for eggs and our father.

# CLOVERS IN THE FIELD

Applause erupted in the school hall as I walked up onto the stage. I was nervous, and it showed in the way my fingers fiddled and pulled at each other.

*Something is wrong.*

At first, it was just a thought that fluttered into my mind that morning, but now it became a nagging voice as I searched the crowd for a familiar face. Mama was there, as always. She beamed with pride as I received my prize, but I looked to her side and saw an empty space.

*Something terrible is going to happen.*

The voice oddly resembled an adult's, but I was just a child when this all took place. Anxiety's root was already embedded in the pit of my stomach, its vines wrapped around my lungs and squeezed when activated by fear.

I decided to concentrate on my prize, an illustrated book about butterflies and why they flew on silent wings. It was a poetically written story that didn't make sense at that time, but it was pretty to look at.

The rest of the class received their certificates, and I clapped ecstatically for my best friends. Next year, we would all meet in high school and in the future, some of us would become acquaintances, but most of us would become enemies.

After the awards ceremony, we said goodbye to my favourite teachers and left my childhood memories in the brick-faced walls of my primary school building. I held Mama's right hand, and my brother held her left as we began to leave the school. To get out, we had to walk down a steep hill, then a flight of stairs guarded by a turnstile gate for the safety of the children.

*This is where my memory gets hazy.*

I'd had a nightmare where Mama was trapped in the turnstile gate. Her arms were tangled painfully between the steel poles meant to allow in human beings, one at a time. My dad stood on the other side, her freedom blocked by his stoutness, as he menacingly twisted the gate and crushed her trapped body. She screamed and screamed until I woke up and realised it was just a dream or an unwanted memory I pushed back into the crevices of my mind. I wasn't sure anymore about differentiating between dreams and memories.

When we finally reached the turnstile gate, I held my breath as Mama pushed through it, and I let out a loud sigh of relief when I saw all her limbs were intact. Our journey was about to continue safely when, suddenly, a car sped into the school grounds and screeched to a halt right next to us. The stench of burnt tyres filled my nostrils, a peculiar smell that would haunt me for the rest of my life.

My dad jumped out of the overheated car, spotted my mummy and approached with a threatening demeanour. People stopped and eavesdropped as my parents began to yell nonsensical words at each other. I don't recall everything that was spat between them, but I remembered this much.

"You must take *your* children and fuck off! I don't want to see you or them in my house!" my father hissed at my mother.

"*My* children? They're your children too! Or did you forget?"

"What the fuck did you tell everyone? I'm losing business because of you!"

"What do you mean because of me? You did this to us and yourself!"

"Fuck you! I want you all out of *my* house!"

"You think I'm dumb? You abandoned us and missed your children's awards day because you were with that bitch! Now, you want us out of our house so you can bring her in? How could you do this to me...to *us*? How could you cheat on me with your fucking secretary!"

This last remark made my dad's hands roll into vein-popping fists. He stalked closer towards Mama like the big cats we watched religiously on National Geographic. I was screaming or crying, one of the only two things I was capable of doing at the age of eleven. My brother was just as helpless, but luckily, his friend's dad stepped in and stopped my father in his tracks, whispering things into his ear. Whatever he said made my dad jump back into his car and drive away, but not without giving my mummy one last look of what I could only describe as utter disgust.

Fear gripped us as a group of mothers surrounded us and comforted Mama. She quivered and wept from the embarrassing, unsettling ordeal. They cooed and invited us home for tea and biscuits, a snack that healed the broken, but my mummy politely declined. With puffy faces and rattling bodies, we resumed our formation, said goodbye to the lovely ladies and continued our walk home.

They say a mother can sense things normal human beings can't, and I believe Mama sensed our growing fear as we journeyed home, so she made a detour. The neighbourhood playground was located between our school and our home: a midpoint and an escape for us.

The grass was well-kept and littered with yellow daisies. It was a beautiful field, but almost always empty. I guessed that all the children had cell phones and other gadgets, so playgrounds and flowers seemed less impressive to them.

Baxter tried hard to hide his disappointment as we walked past the swings and see-saws. He was becoming more aware, and awareness kills innocence. We walked by Mama's side with our heads down until she suddenly stopped. Her eyes were on the sprinklers that showered the field with a drizzle, and I saw a spark of mischief light up her countenance.

"Put your bags over there," she instructed, and we obeyed. My brother and I ran to the corner she pointed at and unburdened ourselves. We knew exactly what she had planned, so we rushed back to her with expectant grins. Mama grabbed our tiny hands and counted down.

"5...4...3...2...1!"

We war-cried in unison and ran into the showering sprinklers. Laughing and dancing together under the fake rain. All the fear, drama, confusion and pain got washed away as we wiggled our arms and twirled carelessly. Our heads lifted towards the sky, and our feet tapped on the wet grass, causing mud to splatter all over our uniforms. Overseers would think we were partaking in some kind of Indian ritual.

This was the last time we would dance under the sprinklers, and we did it until exhaustion hit us. Soaked and out of breath, we sprawled inelegantly under the shade of a giant oak tree. Baxter was picking at the flowers on the ground, gathering them in a messy bouquet and then handing them over to our mummy as she sunbathed.

"Thank you, my son." She peered at each flower and picked one out of the bunch. The next thing Mama did, horrified me.

She smiled sweetly at the green flower and, without warning, popped it into her mouth.

"Mama, you can't eat flowers!" I was wholly disturbed, but she laughed at my reaction.

"Red, some flowers are edible and are meant to be eaten. Even if they're pretty." She turned to Baxter, "Son, find us more clovers and bring them here. The green flowers."

Baxter shot up off the ground and began his search immediately. He was on a mission, and no one could stop him. After a few minutes of scavenging, he came to us with hands filled with the green stuff. Mama thanked him as she took a bottle of water out of her bag and washed the leaves. We sat around her, as silent as our surroundings, with a bunch of clovers in our hands.

"But, Mummy, isn't this a flower for good luck?" I asked concernedly.

"That's a four-leaf clover."

"Will we have good luck forever if we eat the four-leaf one?" Baxter's eyes lit up as we waited for her to answer him.

"Well, there's only one way to find out. Go on, taste it."

My brother and I stared at each other questioningly, then slowly placed a clover on the tip of our tongues. The bitter-sweet taste exploded in my mouth and seemed to travel up my nose to tickle my brain. I pinched my face, and my brother mimicked me.

Meanwhile, my mother's laughter tinkled like a long-lost dream around us. The taste of clover was similar to that of ber.

"I love it!" I exclaimed as I shoved more into my mouth.

"Me too, Ma! It's like sour sweets," Baxter was chewing slowly with his eyes closed, probably imagining he was eating the sweets we bought at Van's Tuckshop.

"I used to eat this all the time when I was a child. Every time your uncles, aunties, and I played outside, we would stop and hunt for clovers. It was like a treat for us." Her eyes glazed over like they usually did when she spoke about her childhood, but she quickly returned to reality.

I couldn't imagine Mama as a child, eating flowers with her brothers and sisters and playing games like stuck-in-the-mud. I could only see her as she was now: defeated by my father, glassy-eyed about her past, and the mask she put on when she remembered she was a mother.

I perceived her with love as we sat in our incomplete circle, cross-legged like we were meditating in the centre of the universe, and chewing slowly on plants, like it was our last meal together. My brother searched frantically for a four-leaf clover in his palm. The urgency of having infinite luck was evident in his darting eyes.

A faint smile tugged at the corners of my mummy's lips as she watched Baxter in his futile exploration. Little did she know that in the years to come, he would still be searching and consuming four-leafed plants with a child-like hopefulness for the luck that came with it. The sounds of the sprinklers came to a stop behind us, signalling the end of the day, but I prayed silently that we could stay there forever.

Eating clovers in the field.

# RAUMATA

The walls of this castle
Bleed with my mother's tears.
The wind doesn't whistle here;
It screams like a woman in labour.
Demons walk freely in and out.
Sulphur fills the air in their presence.
The grass grows rapidly.
Pretty clovers wither away in seconds.
Passers-by look for the beast in our windows.
I have freedom,
Yet, I am trapped.
Suicide is in every room.
Hidden guns are loaded under our beds.
My father's footsteps have no return.
Can I be saved from this wretched scene?
People rush in and look around:
Our abode disgusts them, as it does me.
I see nothing in the darkness,
Clinging mindlessly to the string of hope
For my father's arrival,
For a place of peace,
For a home not filled with Traumata.

# SHEKINAH

## *27th April 2012*

"I looked forward to seeing you today, Red," I said with genuine disappointment.

*Keep it professional, Shekinah.*

"I'm sorry," Red whispered and swiftly continued, "Doctor Shekinah, I was just wondering if I can...maybe send you more of my journals...I mean, my poems and stories? Maybe, through the post?"

I knew if I agreed, this would clash with my profession, but it sounded like a cry for help, and I secretly vowed to assist this child. A few sessions were needed with Red, but there was a time and place for everything. And at that time, Red's place was with her mother.

Being a single mother in a dying economy was taking a toll on Yasmin, and it showed in the vacant look of her eyes, the drastic weight loss and the amount of Xanax she was consuming. My heart broke for her and every suffering mother on Earth.

*It was never in the plan for women to be abandoned by men.*

"That is perfectly fine," I finally responded to Red's question when I felt the coldness of the telephone against my ear. She took down my postal address and softly said her goodbyes before the line went dead.

I would never tell Red this, but I was keen to read the rest of her poems and stories. This was an opportunity for me to dive straight into the human heart of depression and suicide. I had front-row seats to her projected thoughts, which I both hated and loved simultaneously.

*I'm obviously not proud of witnessing my own patient pinpoint when and where her trauma began. That was supposed to be my job.* I scoffed at the thought as I prepared to head home.

I wondered briefly if all humans were self-aware of the source of their pain. Or their *traumata*, as Red put it.

*Do they all hide the knowledge of themselves until they need to be rescued by another being, be it immortal or mortal?*

Even though I desperately wanted to help Red, a little part of me felt like she was already on the right path to finding and helping herself. I pushed aside the fear of impending doom and vanquished the thoughts of one day opening a letter that could possibly be her last one.

*Red is a writer who chronicled her suffering, and I'm just the reader of her sorrows.*

At least, that's how I reassured myself over the next five years as I waited skittishly for her epistles.

*'And you would watch with serenity through the winters of your grief.'*

—Kahlil Gibran, *The Prophet*

# WINTER

## *The Season of Trauma*

# UICIDE

Shrouded in morbid thoughts,
They urge me to speak.
I whisper, cry, scream,
To seemingly deaf ears
Rendered sightless to my pain.
There are no reflections of me,
In the glassy eyes of my friends.
Encased in the darkness of sadness,
This is where I live. This is where I'll die.

# SAD GIRL

"Schizophrenia." The doctor's whisper echoed in the hospital hallway.

"You have to admit her. She could harm herself again." My mother murmured a response that was incoherent from where I sat.

*Schizophrenia.* I heard that word before when they described an aunt of ours. She saw dead people and screamed in her sleep. Her diet consisted only of yellow potatoes and white bread. Despite her reputation, I loved her company because she spoke freely. Unfortunately, women who do this are often unfairly labelled with cruel terms, such as schizophrenic or a witch.

I also admired her storytelling abilities, and her art sketches always gave me the chills, the good kind. She used to weave tales of ghosts and murders straight from her imagination.

*Imagination.* I finally learned the true meaning of that word, as it was the only good thing I had left in my life. My books and my imagination.

My brother and I used to sit and listen religiously to my schizophrenic aunt's stories even though every second word out of her mouth was *fuck* or *fucken.* My father used to say she's just downright crazy.

*If I'm schizophrenic, that means I'm crazy, too.*

A surge of panic hit me as the word finally registered.

*No, I'm not crazy!*

I reassured myself, but doubt gripped me as I heard the

approaching footsteps of my mother and the doctor. My heart pumped so hard that I felt it push against my skin, as if trying to escape. Each beat was more painful than the last. I clutched at my chest to try and stop it from clawing its way out from under my tiny left breast and plopping onto the dirty hospital floor. Forever tainted.

My airways began to shut down, and I struggled to breathe. My mother and the doctor were a few feet away from me, their figures blurred, and their voices seemed miles away. Nobody noticed that I was drowning in plain sight.

*I'm not crazy. I'm not crazy. I'm not crazy. I'm not crazy. I'm not crazy. I'm not crazy.*

"I'm not crazy! I'm not crazy! I'm not crazy! I'm not crazy! I'm not crazy! I'm not crazy!" I wasn't sure if I was screaming this mantra in my head or out loud as a burly African man tried to pick me up off the ground in the hospital parking lot.

"We're just trying to help you, Red," Mum pleaded with a stricken face. People stared at us like it was a show, and I was the entertaining freak. A gust of wind blew out of nowhere and wrapped around my cold, wet face. Making me aware that I was crying. The past few minutes were hazy, and all I knew was that they were taking me to a place where psychotic people go. Maybe it was the adrenaline that kept my body so stiff and heavy on the ground that my mother and the stranger struggled to pick me up.

"I'm not crazy, Ma, please!" I begged and wailed, watching her expressions change.

"I know you're not crazy, but you need help, and I can't help you. The doctors can," she said, feebly.

*How will the doctors heal my mind and heart when they can't even heal the bodies that slowly decay in their beds? How can an empty hospital room fulfil me? How was writing in a journal supposed to help me get rid of the pain embedded in my soul? How did I not die and avoid all of this? How can my own mother not know how to help me?*

I felt nothing but despair and was on the brink of giving up when I heard my mum emit a long sigh.

"Just leave her," she commanded exhaustedly, and the stranger immediately obeyed. He let go of my thin arms, which flopped to the ground and scraped against the tarmac painfully.

"Thank you for trying to help." Mum continued to speak to him as my frantic breathing and crying failed to cease.

The man nodded at her and turned towards the hospital, but hesitated. He seemed lost or unsure of his next step.

Eventually, he circled back to me, bent down on his knees until we were eye-level and spoke softly, "You're going to be okay, trust me." He gently patted my bony shoulder and ventured back into his own life. We didn't even get his name.

Tears cascaded freely down my cheeks, and I didn't care to wipe them away. My mother continued to hover over me, guilt splayed across her face, and I wanted to assure her that none of this was her fault, but I couldn't speak anymore. It seemed like talking about my feelings, thoughts, and emotions only led to catastrophes. So, I decided to keep silent.

"I know you're not crazy." It was a quiet suggestion, but a mother's voice could be heard even in the depths of hell.

"I'm not, Ma," I barely whispered the words as my throat was raw from all the screaming and crying. She held back her tears like she consistently tried to do—months of holding back only to let it all out in the dead of the night. While I pretended to sleep, I heard her lamentations, and if it weren't for that, I wouldn't have known my mother felt as distraught as I did.

"Let's go home." She reached towards me.

*Home? That used to be her*, I mused.

As I steadied my breathing and grabbed her warm hand, I yearned to tell her that the doctor was mistaken. That I wasn't crazy.

I wasn't crazy, even when I bunked school and removed all the knives from the kitchen drawer. I wasn't crazy when I lined them all up and picked the sharpest from the set. The blade sparkled beautifully in the light of the day. I wasn't crazy when I sat on the couch, took a deep breath and sliced easily down my forearm. I wasn't crazy when I watched the blood surge out from my open flesh and then proceeded to do the same to my other forearm. I wasn't crazy when the world went black, and I felt happiness, thinking this sacrifice would bring us back together again.

*Ma, I'm not crazy.*

*I'm just fucking sad.*

# IXTEEN

Girls frolic in elaborate dresses,
Hand in hand, head to chest.
Gentle fathers twirl them,
Around the banquet.
Tears form in our irises,
Never escaping the witnesses.
A show is on for the fatherless,
Parades thrown for daughters,
Sit and observe the love festival.
A frightening celebration for us,
A scarcity for the damned lass
Not registering the hurt
Because the boys stand up.
The boys, *oh* the boys!
And they begin to dance with us;
Recklessly, carelessly, hurtfully.
Pulling and grabbing,
Spinning and toppling,
Stepping on our dainty toes.
Objects of their desires.
As there are no fathers,
Who will dance with us.

# THE BACKROOMS OF SOLITUDE

Chambers, so infinitely black.
A deep-sea swim,
Joining the school of creatures.

In this vast space,
There's an elusive desire to roar,
And to listen to the echoes.

Inky water fills my lungs.
I watch the sky disappear, despairingly,
My dying screech trapped in bubbles.

Life floats to the surface.
Gently bursting in the breeze.
How do I breathe in solitude?

# THE MAN NAMED WINTER

I want to dance carelessly with a blue flame.

Burn my soft fingertips on his sultry, chiselled chin and stare into the pirouetting light until tears drown my eyes.

I do not want to skate on thin ice with a carrot-nosed-button-eyed snowman, my mind focusing only on the blades underneath my clumsy feet, but here I am.

Knees buckling while slow dancing with a man named Winter.

# RIGIDITY

*It's cold*, I thought to myself, *it's so cold.*

I watched the waves dance violently on the lightly littered shoreline; the ferocious rhythm clashed against the scattered debris. The cold seeped into my ear lobes, the tip of my nose, and underneath my fingernails, piercing through my exposed skin. Icicles formed in odd places. They formed on the edge of my hair, the tip of my eyelashes, and around my bony, stiff joints. The frost gripped me and bit deeper with each passing moment. Every inch of my body was captured by it, except one spot.

I sat cross-legged next to him and felt a slight stark contrast to the biting cold. Where our kneecaps touched, a hot spring bloomed, its fragile warmth spread like a gentle flame. The heat radiated through the contact, a tiny but significant barrier against the freezing environment. In that shared warmth, I found solace, a reprieve from the relentless chill in the air and back at home. Therefore, I did not complain about the scarcity of warmth because he provided a minuscule flame between us.

*And a little means a lot to me.*

The silence in our unusual friendship was deafening but familiar to me. The thought of our lips joining never crossed my mind, but in the future, he'll believe that I manifested our kiss, and I'll be accused of seduction.

*A teenage seductress.*

The image of him kneeling before me is etched in my mind forever—a moment suspended in time, vivid and unforgettable.

His posture, a mixture of vulnerability and reverence, spoke volumes without a single word. He leaned in, his eyes searching mine. It was a silent invitation that I couldn't resist, so I leaned closer. Drawn by an invisible force and an undeniable magnetism that pulled us together.

As the distance closed between us, our breaths mingled and created warm puffs of air in the frigid surroundings. The moment our lips met, it was as if a new hot spring had erupted amid the winter sea breeze. It was warm, but I saw no stars, and I heard no fireworks. I was aware of all my senses.

Eyes closed.

Bodies together.

Lips parted.

Warm tongues, minty breaths, a first kiss between two friends, and all that I could think about was, *it's so fucken cold.*

# ABY STEPS

We do not fall in love.
We saunter, heedlessly,
Gradually dancing our way to it
Ever so slowly.

Sirens blare.
Strolling, oblivious.
Nothing but white noise around us
Unexpectedly enamoured.

Never sought,
Never desired,
Not realising a home,
Another mistaken shelter.

We do not fall into love.
No.
We crawl, scrape our knees, wobble,
And walk into love.

# ONLY SEVENTEEN

"My mother loves you. I told her that we're dating. She said you're perfect for me and can't wait for us to start a future together. She also said you're God-sent!" he remarked joyfully.

I shut my eyes, and his mother's image emerged from the darkness of my mind. She stood behind a pulpit a few feet away from me. Her obese body was bathed in a grotesquely bright spotlight. She grinned, and I respectfully smiled back, but the mirage of her got clearer and her grin more devilish.

I frowned and squinted in the dim lighting of my mind as her face slowly distorted in inhumane ways. Her body bent, and cartilages protruded unnaturally. An unmitigated terror gripped me as each fragile bone of her face cracked into a million pieces. The smell of the blood that gushed out of her mouth made me gag.

She tried to say something through the bloody waterfall but spluttered and gurgled instead. I wanted to run away from her, but remembered her son's happiness. After his messy break-up with a 'possessed girl who sang in the church', he was delighted that his mother finally accepted someone.
*God-sent.*

I almost laughed, but that was prohibited in his mother's world. Only devil-worshippers laughed for nothing. I focused back on the vision and saw his father behind the pulpit, too. Preaching his lies whilst stabbing our pastor in the chest.

His mother was still trying to say something to me, but I couldn't hear her from so far away.

I breathed in deeply as I stepped towards her on shaky legs, and I imagined his happiness in the palms of my hands. Each step felt like an eternity until, at last, I stood face to face with the she-devil herself. She and her husband grabbed my wrists so I couldn't run. I resisted and fought back, but my pastor got up from the floor, bloodied and half-dead, and assisted them.

*Why is he helping them after everything?*

His mother searched my face with expectation and then stuttered her words, like a curse, "I...l... lo...love...h... her...f...f...f... for...y... you. For... us."

Spots of blood sprinkled onto my face like an artist's mistake. They let go of my wrists, and I quickly wiped my face with the back of my hand. Their gaze was suddenly torn away from me. Behind me, he stood tall and muscular, listening intently to his mother's wise words and his father's unwise sermons. In a flash of a second, I swore he looked just as distorted as they did, but surely my mind was playing tricks on me.

Abruptly, I remembered his mother's words, and my eyes widened in realisation. I wanted to yell, but my throat felt constricted, stopping the words that wanted to pour out of me.

*But... I'm only seventeen!*

I opened my eyes. The vision disappeared like fog, damned realisation hit me, but instead of denying this unholy relationship, I responded with a shaky voice.

"That's great! I'm glad she approves of me."

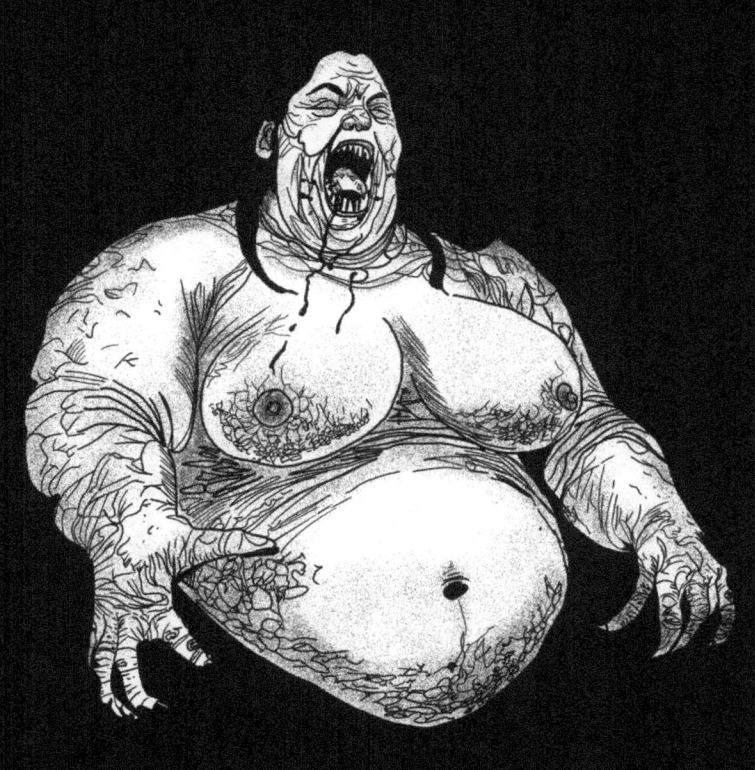

# BUTTERFLY EFFECT

Him.
He is warm,
His arms wrapped me in a consolatory cocoon
Metamorphosing into his beautiful lepidopteran
Destined to be crushed under his big, careless feet.
Hairy, fragile wings scattered like pieces of vellum,
How will I fly now?

# MATRIC DANCE

Black dress, flowering around me.
No lover in a limousine.
Corsage-empty wrists,
Today, I am ready to be seen.

Suit too little for a man so tall,
He arrives in a rusted vehicle
Signs of expectation in his lustful eyes,
And no friends sit at our table.

High prospects of love from an older man,
I patiently wait to be asked to dance.
Across the table, the lovers leave,
But my eyes perceive his folded hands.

Stolen money in a little handbag,
Onto the starchy bed, we both fall
I lay my head pretending to dream.
Because tonight, we *both* won't enjoy the ball.

# TO YOU

You filled my vats until I overflowed.
Then tossed my abundance away,
Settled for unfermented wine,
Stole my disintegrated heart,
Cigarette holes in the tissue,
A heart, too fat, for your hands.
You taught me love, sex, hate,
Abstinence.
You;
Blessed me and cursed me,
Opened me, then closed me to the world,
Held me too tight, to let me go,
Gave me hope but made me hopeless,
Took my hand and left me wondering,
Sent me flowers meant for my coffin,
Bought me things that never lasted,
Showed me a home that was never ours,
Offered peace but left me warring,
Took my innocence, so I felt guilty,
Lobotomised me, then called me crazy,
Snatched my soul so God wouldn't want me.
You.

# OVE IN WINTER

The cold fingertips of a season
Wraps around my head.
Like yours wrapped around my neck,
Life draining out of me.

Remember our winter affair?
Everyone courts in the summer,
You had to be different,
Wrapping me in a brittle embrace.

A false sense of security.
By the dark sea,
A time filled with regrets,
The gale whips at my skin.

Your old, haunting touch
On my youthful face.
Summer love does not last,
A foolish belief is indoctrinated.

Winter is filled with death.
Hopeful fires only exist in Hades.
Cold spots of a lover,
Of his love and his lies.

# ADY QUIETNESS

Quietness was summoned to part her lips.
Wide, she did, in solace.
Her beloved proclaimed,
"Futile speeches are fit only for the trees"

Yet at the sound of her weak voice
The forests rustled their leaves with mirth.
She cast her tale upon the grimy earth,
Like barren seeds

Her secrets blossomed in the soil,
Only for the vermin to feast.
Quietness was summoned to part her lips,
Loud, she did, in solace.

Rivers surged with her screams,
Streams bore her tainted narrative,
Waterfalls wept with her,
Raindrops waltzed upon her words,

Quietness was summoned to part her lips,
The fresh waters, yes, they heeded,
But the healing oceans,
Did not listen.

# DEN

I'm standing in the midst of darkness
Lost in Mother Nature's womb.
Waiting for you to come and whisper
Praises of our dead bloom.

The piercing fingernails of the wind
Claw at my heart,
The bright flame you created
Mere ashes mistaken for art.

I pray the breeze carries my scent,
Follow its trail and enjoy the view.
Call me the Queen of your forest,
I yearn to rule Eden with you.

Now I run wild in this green maze,
Screaming your name.
Lost in the jungle
We were supposed to reign.

# BEEP!

The tub was filled with pink water. Her toes jutted out in the warm pool. Tears mixed with the fragrant bubble bath. Scented candles doused the metallic smell. She feared peeking at the coloured water.

*Would this kill me?* She was hopeful.

Her phone beeped to life on the little wooden table. Its sudden brightness was a sharp contrast to the dim bathroom. She picked it up hazily. The cold outside of the water seeped into her bones, making her movements sluggish. Light from the screen reflected in her exhausted eyes as she unlocked it with a swipe of her finger, her wrinkled touch almost numb against the glass.

Opening the text message, she squinted at the small font, her mind foggy from the hot bath. His name stirred up a familiar feeling within her.

*I'm sorry.* It read.

*Beep!*

Her eyes lit up at the sound of a second text, but that light quickly extinguished when she read it.

*That's a terrible thing to go through alone.*

She watched as his profile picture disappeared, his busy status turned into cyber nothingness, and the water turned red as he left her alone with all her terrible, terrible things.

# ISSING

She wishes she had heard a heartbeat.
Or witnessed an eerie image on a screen.
Trying to guess with her lover,
Each part of the body.

But God only offered her a glimpse
Of an incomplete vessel.
All she could touch was skin
That's supposed to be alive.

Innocent blood on her fingertips.
She smelled a sweet life drain away,
And tasted the sourness of death.
The truth of femininity was revealed.

She never knew real heartbreak,
In all the years that preceded her womb.
A mini version of love rotted in a small grave,
And her baby was never coming home.

# EXISTENTIALISM

I learned something profound in high school. First, I'd like to explain where I learned this profound thing. On the far side of my high school building, there was a flight of stairs where the delinquent girls bunked classes and smoked cheap cigarettes. Down these stairs, deep within the bowels of the school and so far removed from the rest of the classrooms that we had to sprint to our next lesson, was where Dramatic Studies was held.

I called it hell, but the other girls called it the basement. It was dark and damp, and the teacher matched the room. She was an atheist, you see, and you can imagine what she imparted to us in the dungeon of our high school.

One morning, she handed out books to each student. It was a play. I won't mention the name of the play as I don't wish to encourage the reader of my journal to seek it out, but trust me, it will transform you.

In this play, there was a man who waited for a man who, quite possibly, never existed. The waiting man encountered strangers who questioned his pursuit of an invisible being, but he remained steadfast in his spot under a tree, waiting for nothing. I don't recall all the minute details of the play, but one thing struck me after reading it, and my teacher confirmed what I was thinking when we shut the books and handed them back to her.

The classroom was filled with susurrations when she said, "Life is meaningless."

Silence enveloped us as we listened to her sermonise about the non-existence of a higher being: no God, no devil and no meaning to this painful life. Imagine my shock in hearing that everything I am going through and have gone through is abolished in the black hole of nothingness.

Every day, on my way home from school, I remembered contemplating the meaninglessness of life.

*But doesn't that mean that even thinking about how meaningless life is, is in fact, meaningless too?*

I watched as my right foot stepped before my left and vice versa. I observed as my long skirt billowed in the hot wind, and the arguments with my mother about wearing shorter skirts like the popular girls. I studied my fingers as they brushed against my sides. I focused on walking properly so the boys wouldn't mock me.

*Meaningless.*

At my gate, my dogs greeted me with their usual jumps and inexplicable joy at my presence. Their ribs jutted visibly like mine. My parents were incapable of feeding them, too. My little brother was out on some adventure with his friends, running barefoot through the neighbourhood, getting called names like hobo or beggar-child. His heart soared with a freedom they would never understand, just as I couldn't.

*Meaningless.*

I couldn't cook, so we starved until my mother came home from her low-paid, overworked, good-for-nothing job to prepare a paltry meal that ended up half-eaten. My mother never ate with us, not since my father left. She lost so much weight that people started rumours saying that she had AIDs. My parents were well-known in the community, but these strangers and gossipers didn't understand true sadness.

65

True sadness ate my mother and made my brother run free in the night, like a wolf or a monster. Either one, it didn't matter.

*Meaningless.*

The knowledge of clitoral orgasms at the age of six. The cute boy who drugged and molested me with his dirty fingers at the age of fifteen. A college student next to our high school who preyed on me and other sixteen-year-olds. The older man I was in love with, who begged me for my virginity as soon as I turned eighteen. The pungent regret mixed with the blistering pain between my thighs.

Sex and sexuality.

Rape and molestation.

Men and boys.

*Meaningless.*

The fresh scars on my arms. The wind in my hair. God, aliens and humanity. My father's affairs and my mother's oppression. My brother's lost childhood. Our abandonment. Our starvation. Our house. My bed, stained with blood from my wrists. Suicide and love. All and everything were absurd, inconsequential, nonsensical, trivial, insignificant, and negligible.

Like the man who waited for a man who quite possibly never existed.

*Meaningless.*

# SHEKINAH

*17th May 2017*

*Oh, shit! Not existentialism!*
The letterbox clanged loudly and echoed in my silent neighbourhood. Another month and no word from Red, her last letter sent a cold shiver down my spine, and the empty post box proved that something was wrong. Five years of writing, and all of a sudden, she stopped.

Even though there were long gaps between receiving Red's poems and stories, her last letter arrived in the middle of last year, and by now, I should have received more. The sense of dread intensified when I called her and Yasmin, but both calls went straight to voicemail.

*Damn technology.* I realised that after all these years, their numbers would have changed.

My thoughts briefly drifted to Isa, my brother. A sharp pang of longing for him struck me when I began reading Red's journal and letters. Although our father had stayed, he was always too busy helping the strangers who sought his healing, leaving us to understand Red's predicament. Isa would have cherished reading her poetic words about Baxter, but she had entrusted me with them, and I would never betray a young woman's trust.

He, too, would have understood Baxter's silent ache and how it felt to become a man without his father's guidance. A father is someone who should be there when you need him the most, but our father put others first. I coped with the pain by helping others who shared in it, while Isa wept and wrote beautiful librettos for the world to hear. I glanced at Red's letters, and a sudden idea struck me.

*Dear Red,*

*Where do I begin?*
*Writing is your forte and definitely not mine. I usually leave the letter writing to my secretary, but this felt too personal and important to pass it on to someone else.*
*I am writing because it has been so long since I've heard from you. I tried calling you and your wonderful mother, too.*
*How is she? She is always on my mind.*
*And how is your brother, Baxter? He sounds phenomenal. Did I tell you that I have a brother, too?*
*I think I have grown accustomed to your letters, and now it worries me that you haven't been writing anymore.*
*Are you okay?*
*I hope you know that I am not just here to read but also to listen. I guess I am trying to say that I care deeply about you and your life. Your last letter mentioned existentialism, and I am not against that belief, but please remember that there are real, tangible things out here that love and care deeply about you. I am one of them.*
*I can probably get into a lot of trouble for this in my profession, but I'm pretty sure that the rules don't matter anymore because*

*I consider you my sister and friend.*
*I only have one request, which is for you to continue writing,*
*even if you never send it to me. I have a feeling that your words*
*will find their way to the world, the heavens, and me someday.*

*I will always be here.*

*Yours truly*
*Shekinah*
*17th May 2017*

*Dear Dr. Shekinah,*

*My family is well, thank you for asking.*
*I think I am well, too, as I am still alive. ( I know you just*
*secretly wanted to see that I have never taken to the knife again,*
*but thank you for caring. ) There is no knife in my hands*
*nowadays, only a pen.*
*I was surprised to find out that you have a brother. I always*
*thought you were an only child. I felt guilty about writing to you*
*because you have this beautiful life, and here I am, tainting it*
*with my morbidity.*
*It didn't feel right to dump my trauma on you, and yet you*
*wrote to me for more. Your letter made me smile.*
*I know my last letter was about existentialism, but I am at a*
*time in my life where I'm struggling to believe in a higher power.*
*I can tell you one thing, though. If there is a God then He*

*definitely sent you.*

*This may surprise you, but after the last story I wrote, I have been studying theology. This journey started as a personal one. I was just trying to find God and the meaning of life in all this mess, but then it got out of control and branched off to preaching and singing in a church choir. This is why I haven't been writing to you.*

*I am not proud to say that I stood at a pulpit without belief, preaching words that still don't make sense to me. The church looks at me like I'm some prophetess touched by the Lord Himself, but to be honest with you, I just loved the attention I was getting.*

*I won't give too much away in just a simple letter. I'm sure you have now found my poems and stories in the envelope. Please read them.*

*To know that someone out there reads my story is more than enough for me, but you went above and beyond by caring, too. For that, I could never thank you enough. I hope to see you soon, but until then, I will keep on writing to you.*

*Your sister and friend,*
*Red.*
*25th May 2017*

*'When you love you should not say, "God is in my heart," but rather, "I am in the heart of God."'*

—Kahlil Gibran, *The Prophet*

# UTUMN
## *The Season of Spirituality*

![full-page illustration]

# OG SHIT

I had a lover who walked around the church hall with salvation on his collar and pride in his lifted chin... always greeting people with a daft smile and that deep, misleading dimple as he sang praises in unholy pitches for the starry-eyed congregation. The pulpit was his shooting ground because he could easily spot the female victims whilst his family sat, protected from their son's bullets. Self-righteously, like dirty and unwanted weeds, they grew their roots within the foundations of the temple, which would later destroy God's house.

All the men in self-proclaimed power imagined his importance and wondered what on Earth he was doing with a pauper like me. Surely, he deserved a woman *filled with the Spirit.* A lady who carried herself with grace but forgot all gracefulness when she worshipped the good Lord. Abandoning her clothes as she danced like David before God's throne. Women who were weak and quiet and cried a lot in the choir during hymns were unacceptable for marriage, and I was one of them.

Flaws in the church were a sin. You had to walk like you did not have any flaws. Walk like you did not sin. That was his secret and theirs. Flawed women were dubbed possessed by him and his family—me, my mother, and his ex.

So, he walked around the church with his eyes averted from the crowd and straight ahead as if God stood before him. He walked with power, or that is what he believed. On the other hand, I walked with shame, as he continuously pointed out. My eyes were permanently lowered, giving him the power to preach about my beauty to me. He hoped that I'd lift my head up and never drop my gaze again, but it's funny, I never thought I was ugly until I met a man of God. My thoughts didn't matter because he believed beautiful women should always look up.

*How will I see where I'm walking if I always look up?*

I wanted to argue with him, but I couldn't. I had no evidence to plead my case. He was bigger and stronger, and he had lived longer than I, which automatically made him wiser. I just thought he was a massive cunt that God unfairly favoured for some reason. But my thoughts didn't matter.

He claimed to love me like God, and I believed him. A new fear was unlocked when I learned that Satan was the father of lies, and, oh, how my man of God lied to me. After him, I would have much rather signed a contract with an incubus than a real man, especially the men who lifted their hands in worship.

*Men and God.*

I got the two mixed up, and that's where I went wrong. It wasn't how I walked that was incorrect; it was my disillusionment with who I was walking with.

After skipping another Sunday service, I sat back on my sofa and imagined a world filled with people walking just like him. Heads up, shoulders down, back straight and eyes always straight ahead. Never looking down.

Yes, this was the world he envisioned.

A world filled with beautiful people trampling all over dog shit.

# USED TO SING

I used to sing,
In the church, up front.
I used to worship God,
And watch the people pull a stunt.
But it was all a lie.
For I am a sinner, you see,
And the church cannot accept
A singer who is free.

# NHOLY FIRE

Taken into the pack
On holy grounds.
The Wolves licked my wounds,
And made me whole.
The perfect sacrifice has no flaws.
Omega taught me the language of the gods,
Alpha filled my void,
But, oh, the Beta.
Protector of my soul
Who led me to Hades.
To watch my soul burn,
To open the wounds, he lovingly kissed,
To bury me alive next to their true god.
Come, witness my betrayal.
Unearth me.
Find them in the holy places.
They hide behind God,
And howl for the devil.
For the love they give
Comes from unholy fire.

# SUICIDAL GOD

*Is suicide permissible if God did it?*

Whispered thoughts reverberated like the echo of church bells in my mind, which was shadowed by depression. The human psyche often drifted towards God, His son and the Holy Spirit. A triune entity. Three in one.

"Three's company," as they say. And yet, we deny the existence of celestial beings veiled from our frail vision. Human eyes are useless. The voices in our heads are misinterpreted for our subconscious, or perhaps our subconscious misidentified as the divine trilogy?

This holy trilogy, so meticulously explained: one we should not blaspheme, one we should not provoke, and one we are to love, who in turn overflows with such boundless love that He lived, died and lived anew for our sake: a miracle, a sacrifice, a zombie God.

*Was God too much, too boundless, that He needed to split Himself? Or was His solitude so vast that He sought His own companionship?*

I often envisioned God when he crafted flawed creatures in His own image, infusing them with free will like an essential spice in His cosmic concoction.

"Yep, this is good," He declared whilst retreating to His ethereal paradise.

The newborn beings, already adults at the moment of creation, found themselves thrust into the world, bewildered by the Earth and the animals around them. If their eyes opened any wider from their shock, it would escape the confines of the skulls they barely knew they possessed. Imagine how their minds reeled from the astonishment of suddenly existing.

"Aaaaaah! What the fuck! What am I?"

"Who am I? Who are you? What are we meant to do here? What is my purpose?"

"How did we come to be?"

"What is this place?"

"Who brought us here?"

"Why?"

"Who?"

"What?"

"Where?"

"Who is God, and where is He?"

*Sound familiar?* Lost beings implored lost beings while God remained distant. He observed with silent awe and hoped that one day, despite the fact that they couldn't see Him, touch Him or sense Him, they would seek and worship Him wholeheartedly. From the inception of time, God's omnipotence separated Him from us, the lowly creation. We were deemed unworthy to gaze upon His countenance, and yet we were ranked above the Angels. It's no wonder they rebelled.

A myriad of winged eyeballs and grotesque yet sublime creatures assembled to attack an omnipotent and all-loving God. War erupted within the heavens. Leviathans surged through paradise, biting the heads off Michael and Gabriel.

These were futile attacks, for their torn sinews and ruptured flesh seamlessly wove back together, and new heads emerged as effortlessly as rising helium balloons. Invincible, terrifying beings clashed, slashed, gnashed, and tore at one another with primal fury.

*Of course, if they had advanced weaponry, this war would have unfolded quite differently in my imagination.*

The point is this: a portion of God's creation, one-third of the Angelic host, to be exact, aligned themselves under a singular aim. To overthrow God.

*But why?* That was a question I would have asked at the beginning of time.

*Why did the Angels listen to Lucifer and agree? What words did he speak to sway one-third of them against a deity who was omniscient, omnipotent, omnipresent, loving, merciful, and ever-forgiving? And more importantly, what could God have possibly done to piss them off?*

Had God been a woman, I'd have resented Her for creating men—the progenitors of violence, rape, and murder. I would have loathed Her for the agony of childbirth and for making beauty an obsessive ideology amongst us. I would have been repulsed by Her reluctance to acknowledge the evil in the world She had shaped with Her own hands. But alas, God is not a woman.

He is a man created by men, and when men are in charge, they commit atrocities. Their gravest errors are cloaked beneath the veil they claim is God's wrath. In all honesty, if God were just a father, then that's simply not enough for me. And if He were both male and female, it would confuse the ideological battlegrounds of this era.

But picture this: what if God was not defined by gender or

form, neither male nor female, nor even a face? What if God were a non-descript entity, a higher being made of light? One who doesn't own time but is time. A photon that captured every infinitesimal moment of our existence and engraved it into the fabric of the universe. An electromagnetic energy that would blind us if we dared to gaze at Him/Her/It/They.

"Let there be Light. Let there be more of Me. I shall breathe my life into this universe. Through My words, I shall create!" *Bang!* Homo sapiens and taxes were created.

Would it be a surprise to discover that God was merely a reflection on the ocean's surface, or the light of dawn breaking through the horizon, or the searing sun rays in the heart of a desert? Would it be a disappointment if God were just the thing that brought the colour of our skin to life and revealed our sins by casting us beneath His unrelenting spotlight?
*I don't know.*
There's only one certainty that remains. God could manifest as anything beautiful and pleasing to soothe our aesthetically driven minds. But what if He was none of these lovely things at all?
*What if God was bad?*
An egocentric narcissist who insisted the world orbit around Him, lest He throw a divine tantrum and burn it all to ash. Through suffering, His pets (that's us) must continue our worship despite the absence of His aid or mercy. Perhaps we were nothing more than God's most cherished failed experiment, a Tuesday night drama He indulged in, week after week, projected onto an eternal screen. False suspense played in His mind while He waited for us to make preconceived

decisions in our lives, and for His own amusement, all the choices were wrong.

*I mean, look at that poor guy, Job.*

"Yo, God! Let's fuck with that guy, Job." Lucifer suggested with a diabolical grin.

"Uh, why? And who allowed you back in here? Didn't I kick you out? Gabriel!"

"Woah there! There's no need to summon my crazy brother. Just hear me out, okay? We fuck around a little bit with Job, just a bit, to see if he genuinely loves you. After all, no one truly loves you if all you ever do is shower them with kindness and fulfil all their desires, right? So, it's just a  test to see if his devotion to you is sincere."

"Hmm... I'm intrigued. Continue, Serpent!"

*Who, honestly, is God? I pondered.*

*Male? Female? Neither? Are there three, and why is it sinful to acknowledge them separately? Where do I, a woman, fit in this holy patriarchal structure? And why did God deliberately orchestrate the death of His own son?*

*His son, who is, paradoxically, Himself. And He who is His son. The omniscient God, who was fully aware that His own son was going to die, yet allowed it without divine intervention. And if God's son is indeed Himself, then in that act, He committed the ultimate transgression.*

God committed suicide.

# ISTORTED REFLECTIONS

Mirrors, still waters,
Refractions of our essence, multiplied.
The spirit obscured,
Visages are our souls.

We discern no profundity.
Yet, men dive ceaselessly into us,
Probing our riverbeds,
Destroying our ecosystems.

The search for God
Nestled within the depths of women.
We can only descend,
We cannot soar to Him.

Distorted reflections.
Ripples create monstrous identities,
Each mirror yields a clone.
Our true self, beyond recognition

OSSESSED

*God may not be real, but the Devil is.*

Our pastor sequestered the sisters in the lounge beneath the peeling, water-stained ceiling. The ladies babbled incoherently in an unknown language. An inexplicable strength overtook their limbs as they wrestled with the pastor and Baxter. They kicked and cackled like malevolent witches. Fear never gripped my brother or me, but curiosity did.

*The Devil is here, but where is God?*

The pastor prayed fervently, anointing their foreheads with consecrated olive oil as the sisters writhed and screamed inhumanely. Their eyes rolled back within their skulls, and the older sister began to gag. I ran to fetch a bucket. She heaved over the rim, retching violently as the pastor's prayers persisted. My brother held down the younger sister, whose unearthly wails echoed throughout the house.

"No! No! No!" she yelled, or *it* yelled.

At last, the older sister threw up her contents, and the sound of something solid hit the bottom of the bucket.

*Liquid doesn't thud,* my curiosity piqued.

She passed out beside the bucket, a trail of blood oozed from her lips, and the pastor's wife bent to comfort her for her loss. I edged towards the bucket and peered inside. There, at the bottom, lay something that resembled a wooden log. It was about the size of my forearm and pulsated with life. I stared at the thing and wondered how she harboured it in her minuscule body.

*Fascinating*, I thought.

My attention returned to the younger sister, who continued to scream and grew exceptionally violent. I figured that the Devil sensed oncoming defeat and decided to fight with desperation as palpable as his malice. The pastor continued his battle, and I couldn't help but wonder why God remained silent and invisible while Satan manifested himself in logs and tortured women. I was furious.

The younger sister began to vomit in the bucket, too—no logs this time, just bile and food. Later, we would discover that her co-workers had cast a spell on her, poisoning her with ashes. This malefic art is known as 'black magic' or 'muthi'. Two Indian women, Rajeshrie and Sarah, both mothers and wives, had sought to ruin another mother and wife out of jealousy.

*I hope they burn in hell.*

My mind itched with anger as I watched the sisters writhe in pain on the cold, tiled floor. A sense of calm filled the room in the aftermath of their deliverance, and silence flooded the house. The pastor and his wife cleaned up the Devil's mess, and a new fear unlocked inside of me as I realised an unsettling truth: even in the spiritual realm, women are not safe. Our bodies, minds, and now our souls can be taken without consent, like the Devil took hold and refused to leave the sisters' vessels, draining their lives and leaving them feeling unwanted and dirty. Our bodies and souls are victims of rape.

But demons aren't necessary to make women feel like detritus. No, they already have their husbands, fathers and brothers who did the job just as well, if not better. Whether they were delivered from men or demons, these were the type of women I idolised. Damaged women whose vessels were invaded by someone or something, and yet they still stood tall. Sanity or insanity. God or no God. On that exorcist day, I learned something new: that there was no difference between demons and men. And that women could endure the evils of both.

# Incubus

He visits at night
Announced by the sting of sulphur.
Blankets peeled back,
Mature bodies laid bare,
Faceless in the dark.

Claw marks on pale thighs,
Blooming bruises on tender skin,
"Where did they come from?"

Prayers rise, a plea for salvation,
"God show mercy on the impure!"
In a bed defiled by evil
The demon plants its seed.
No light lingers in her eyes.

The end draws near,
A woman's cry, cut short.
As the Incubus comes hither.

# RAGGED TO HELL

### *Red*

It was still bright outside when Baxter fell into a deep slumber on the couch. He napped for what seemed like half an hour and awoke with a shock. His eyes bulged in fear and pain as he jumped off the sofa and frantically touched the back of his shirt.

"Am I bleeding?" He spun towards me, panic in his expression as he checked his hands.

"No, why?" My eyes swept over him, but I found no traces of blood.

I was utterly puzzled by his sudden wakefulness and, even more so, by the story he proceeded to tell. I would've written our conversation word for word, but a story of this nature should be written from the protagonist's perspective.

### *Baxter*

I found ashes in my wardrobe. My father's uncle was the only guest who stayed over, but even before that incident, I never felt safe in my bedroom. I was never alone in there. Something or someone lurked within the shadows and pounced on my chest when I slept. So, I slept on the couch.

*No peace for the wicked*, the whispered verse echoed violently against the walls of my mind. My skeletal body sank comfortably into the thick cushions, and the blanket was heavy but cosy.

*Maybe I'm not that wicked.* I chuckled as I felt the weight of a deep sleep pull on my eyelids. It was wishful thinking, but I already knew the truth about who I was. It was sleep that overtook me, but peace never accompanied it. As my body continued to sink, I sighed from the satisfaction of finally resting.

*I hope my dreams will be of God,* I silently prayed.

I remembered the brightness that seeped through our white curtains and reddened my vision behind closed eyelids. I remembered the dread I felt when that red was slowly replaced with darkness, and I continued to sink. My eyes flew open to see a receding tunnel of light above me. The cushions and blanket seemed to melt around my body like marshmallows in a fire.

The more I struggled, the more it entangled me. I opened my mouth to scream, but no sound escaped my lips. Instead, the last of my breath gushed out as the materials suffocated me. I was drowning in air and blankets and fought the thoughts that something was about to sit on my chest, and this time, I wouldn't be able to fight it or escape. I felt my pulse slow down as I continued to descend into the quicksand that was my sofa just a few minutes ago.

*This is it, I'm dying.*

A part of me felt at peace with the fact that I was dying, but another part wished for more time. Time for love and time to be loved. I longed to prove to my mother that I was not a failure and to my father that I would never be like him. I yearned to see God and His miracles in the land of the living, but it was all futile. As death pulled me into his depths, I accepted my fate.

89

Suddenly, I felt my back protrude through a hole at the bottom of the quicksand couch, and cold air brushed against my exposed skin.

*A way out!*

Adrenaline possessed me as I wiggled with all my strength until my legs were set free and dangled in the air. I felt no floor below, but that didn't matter as I used the last of my strength to push through this torture.

*Please, God!*

My brain felt like it was about to explode from the lack of oxygen, but with one last shake, I fell through the hole and landed painfully on a cold, rocky and wet ground.

"Fuck!" I yelled, and it echoed in the vast space. I got up and dusted myself off as I took in my surroundings.

"What the fuck is this place?"

The world before me felt unnatural. It was grey and stank like shit and death. The stench reminded me of the day I found a dead rat under our front porch. I pinched my nose and adjusted my eyes to the blackness beyond. At the far end of what I assumed was a cave, a slit of flickering light reflected off a wall.

"Where there's light, there's people," I whispered, ignoring the strange feeling in my stomach as I ran towards it. My feet sank into the ground and made a sickening squelching sound. Halfway to my destination, a woman's blood-curdling scream stopped me in my tracks.

"Where are you?" I cried out.

My eyes darted to and fro, but the shapes in the shadows were just rock formations. There was an eerie silence when the echo of my voice died down. I heard murmurs coming from the light and decided it would be wiser to get help first and then search for the mysterious woman. I ran as fast as I could to the light and found, to my amazement, that it was escaping from the crack of a massive, red, intricately engraved French door.

*Damn, must be rich motherfuckers.*

Beyond the door, the murmurs grew louder until I heard a cacophony of voices. They spoke in a language I didn't understand, and their words made my skin crawl. The sounds of loud chewing were mixed with their outlandish dialect. I was tempted to slip through the open door, but something made me hesitate.

Instead, I treaded softly to the opening and slowly peeked inside. What I witnessed petrified me. Flames danced on sticks, and little bonfires were scattered on the floor. In the middle of the room was a long table with a woman's naked body, and I watched in horror as demonic creatures devoured her—piece by piece.

*I'm in hell.*

I couldn't tear my eyes away from the demons that castrated and chewed noisily on that woman's flesh. They spoke as they ate, and I realised the scene was oddly familiar.

*The Last Supper.*

My nostrils flared as they mocked my God. I tried to guess the names of the demons from one side of the table. Each of them resembled a mix of animals, humans and something ungodly. Some had hooves, and others had wings, but none of them were beautiful. I made a game out of it and tried to find Lucifer.

My gaze slid expectantly along the line of dining demons. I scrunched my face in disgust as one ripped open the woman from her private area to her stomach and gobbled the entrails that fell out. I was so engrossed by the scene that I never realised I had stepped closer to the door.

When I finally averted my attention, I saw the demon in the middle staring back at me. His eyes were poisonous green, and gazing into them filled me with an overwhelming sense of dread. Ten long horns, like those of a bull, jutted out from his seven heads, and each horn was adorned with a jewelled crown.

His face was charcoal black, and his mouth had rows of sharp teeth. He was majestic in an unholy way and towered above the rest of them. All the demons around him abruptly stopped feasting and sat upright, their backs straight and heads forward. Silence enveloped the room.

*The Beast.*

"Fuck this!"

My legs moved on their own accord, and I ran blindly through the cavern. I tripped on rocks and ran into sculptures. These delays caused the Beast to catch up. His thunderous steps were frightening as he closed in on me. I could see his animalistic form at the corner of my eye as I stumbled along an unseen path. I ran as fast as possible, but it was not fast enough.

I heard the ripping sounds of clothes and flesh. Knives or claws raked my back, and I fell to the ground. I howled in pain and tried to crawl away from the heat of the demon behind me. I felt his shadow hover over me in the darkness, and I asked God for forgiveness as he lifted his arm and began clawing my back to shreds.

### *Red*

"Red! Check my back!" Baxter's booming voice snapped me back to reality after listening to that haunting dream of his.

*Or was it a vision?*

I frantically nodded at him as he hissed in pain and peeled his shirt off. When he exposed his back to me, I clasped my hands over my mouth to hold in the scream that bubbled in my throat. I refused to scare him even more.

"Is it bad?" He looked over his shoulder, and my stricken expression answered him. Baxter rushed to the mirror.

"What the fuck!" He turned in every direction, not believing his reflection.

I ran to the bathroom and wet a towel. The running water was a soothing distraction. When I returned, he was sitting on the edge of a chair, his head bowed like he was utterly defeated. I sat opposite him and passed him the towel, which he tentatively took and wrapped around his upper body, wincing at the contact. We stayed like that for a while before Baxter finally looked at me with wounded eyes.

He heaved heavily, and his skeletal body rattled before he asked this indelible question with a shaky, low voice, "Do you think God was there?"

I eyed my brother wearily; his vision plagued my mind, but the answer to his question was clear.

"How would you have escaped hell if God wasn't with you?"

# HE DIVINE ARTIST

The searing blaze of the Sun
Cradles us in Winter's clutch.
Moonlight, the mere reflection.
Eves never fully darkened.

Infinite stars litter the skies,
Asteroids veer from Earth's path.
Ringed planets orbit our Sun.
A universe within a universe.

Innumerable grains along the shore.
Freshwaters sate our thirst,
Soil that breathes life into seeds,
Our needs, met by Mother Nature.

Creatures enrich our land and hearts.
A harvest prepared for our hunger.
Undeniably, Earth was well-wrought,
By the gentle hands of The Divine Artist.

# HE ABYSS

Darkness envelops my sight.
Lost without the sun's warm guidance.
*Is this place called home?*
I ponder.

I feel alive when I am not seen,
Walking within the shadows of God.
Freedom comes in the night
Like the wave of a black ocean.

I drown in the absolute abyss.
All breath has been erased,
Looking up into nothing,
I find hope in everything.

# VE AND THE DEVIL

"Did God *really* say that?"

Eve desperately looked around for Adam but failed to find him within the sentinel trees of the beautiful garden. She had come to gather fruit, to feel the world with her hands, to taste life — but instead, she found the serpent.

"God said we may eat the fruit of any tree except the one that stands in the centre of the garden. If we eat the fruit from that tree, we would die." Eve's gaze drifted across the garden to *that* tree, which glowed like God when He walked with Adam.

The fruits swelled upon its limbs as if they were alive, like her, and each leaf was a different hue of green. A gust of wind blew through her hair, and she closed her eyes as she listened to the sound of a million rustling leaves. Eve was so lost in the beauty of creation that she never realised the creature had crawled closer to her.

"That's not true, you won't die," the serpent whispered, "God fears that you may become like Him. Eyes open, mind awakened, knowing both good and evil."

Eve glanced at the tree again and back at the serpent, who smiled cunningly at her.

*What if the serpent is telling the truth?* She saw how beautiful the tree was and how tasty the fruit looked.

*Why would God forbid something that looks so beautiful?*

Eve made her way to the tree, which seemed to call her, and picked a fruit. Before she could think about it, she bit into it.

The sweet juices filled her mouth and dripped down her naked body. She shut her eyes and moaned in ecstasy. The forbidden fruit's sweetness unravelled her taste buds and her thoughts. It was the best fruit she had ever tasted in the garden, and she had to tell Adam. As Eve plucked more fruit from the tree, the serpent watched with glee from the bushes.

*I have to take these to Adam.*

Eve stopped suddenly and dropped all the fruits.

*What have I done? Why does everything feel...different?*

She looked at the mess around her bare feet and gasped.

"I'm naked!" Eve's hands covered her breasts, and she suddenly felt hot.

*Why am I naked? Is this what it means to be like God? And why am I here?*

Eve was unsure why her breathing increased and her breasts heaved frantically under her palms. Her skin prickled, hypersensitive to the world around her, and for the first time, she became aware of her own body in a way that felt exposed, raw, and deeply personal. She searched around the garden and found some fig leaves, which she fashioned around her to cover her nakedness. Once she was covered, she calmed down, but her thoughts continued to dance around haphazardly.

Eve picked another armful of fresh fruit from the tree and walked away from the garden's magnetic centre. Adam and God would be furious with her, but she didn't care about them because the feelings and thoughts that plagued her overwhelmed her fear. She couldn't make sense of what was happening to her, only that something had changed irrevocably. And when her thoughts suddenly wandered back to the day she was formed, sculpted from a man's rib, created to ease his loneliness, she heaved from the shock of her reality.

"Was I created from him *just* for him?" she yelled to the trees, the garden, and God, but nothing and no one had responded. "I need answers!"

Her brow began to sweat, and tears fell from her eyes as she remembered nights of nakedness with Adam. Lying with him innocently as his hands roamed her body, while she submitted without understanding.

*Does God have more than that planned for me?*

She wanted more, no, she *needed* more than Adam, sex, and a garden. More than the purpose of being a companion to a man made from dust.

*But is there more to me than just a body created to conceive for man?*

Eve was perplexed and haunted by the endless questions. One thing was for sure: she had to keep this from God. She knew that what she did was wrong. The fruits in her arms felt heavy, so Eve laid them on the ground and sat next to them, allowing her mind to adjust to the changes.

*Where is the serpent?* She looked around, but the creature was long gone, and Eve knew she had been tricked. She looked at one of the fruits, which still seemed alive and temptingly delicious.

"If this is what God feels and thinks, then He is unbearably lonely. I can't imagine knowing everything and not having someone to share it with," Eve spoke to one of the fruits and thought she saw it react, but quickly dismissed it as a trick of her eye.

Despite the trickling feeling of dread, Eve felt excited about discovering what was good and evil. She hoped that God would give her more to do, like Adam. Now that she understood God more and became like Him, maybe He would be proud of her decision to eat the fruit and gain knowledge. She smiled and lay on her back, staring up at the towering trees. Eve didn't want to have knowledge of everything alone, like her lonely God did. So she decided that Adam would eat the fruit, and then he could discover the truth, too.

*And he would know me like I now know myself.*

"Is that why God made us?" she wondered aloud. "Because He was alone, with no one who knew Him, no one to grasp the weight of all He held inside. No one to help him carry the burden of all the knowledge of good and evil. No one to tell him that He has the potential to be more than what He knows?" She turned to the fruit, its skin glistened as if it were listening.

"Well then... I refuse to be lonely like God. I will give you to the man, he will enjoy your juices, as I did, and he will gain knowledge of good and evil. Together, we will understand God... and perhaps, in doing so, ease the burden He's carried alone for who knows how long. We will be like God, but unlike Him, we will have each other. No more solitude in knowledge. No more isolation in understanding.

"Because of me, a woman, neither God nor man will remain alone in what they know. And we will know what is good and set aside all that is evil. God will be proud of my independent decision and my courage. He will surely bless me for seeking to understand Him and desiring to share in His truth. He will love me still, as He always has. And most importantly, He will finally walk beside *me* in the garden."

Eve rose to her feet, brushed the dust from her brown skin, picked up the fruits from the ground, and stepped into Eden in search of Adam.

# IN IS A WOMAN

In the eyes of the Saints
How great a sinner she is.
Not just by name.
But by her mere existence as well.
She walks into the room glowing,
With the light of God
But veiled eyes only see darkness.
Self-proclaimed gods on Earth.
"But where is your throne?" she queries.
With anger, the saints pick up stones,
Ready to purge her invisible demons.
Devils, only they can see in her.
Blood will not be on their hands,
God wipes their murders away
With the cloth of forgiveness.
Forgotten blood of a sinful woman.
For their holiness surpasses their evil deeds.
"Let's stone her to death"
At the sight of their anger
She surrenders to death
But Life interrupts the scene,
Writing Love into the Earth.
He speaks words of the Spirit,
"If you are without sin, cast the first stone."
Pebbles fall to the ground
At the feet of sinning saints.
You see, Sin is a woman whom God set free.

# SHEKINAH

**28th March 2020**

*Hi Doctor!*

**Red, we've been through this. Please call me Shekinah.**

*Sorry, Hi Shekinah!*

**Lol, that's much better!**

*It's weird texting you after all the unconventional ways we've been communicating.*

**I know, I wish we had a choice in this matter**

*Me too! How crazy is time? Just last month, I was celebrating my crown birthday with my loved ones, and now we're all caged in our houses and sending you a letter might actually kill you.*

**A plague…imagine. I'm still processing it too!**

*A freaking plague! We have seen it all... The*
*only thing that would surprise me now*
*is the rapture.*

**Oooh! You should write a poem about**
**the rapture.**

*Most poets write about the end. I enjoy the middle*
*of everything. Pain, suffering, love, and life.*
*The middle is where the story lies*
*and where poems are birthed*

**Poetry is in birth and death, too, don't you think?**
**Like how you were born to be a poet.**

*Yes, but birth and death are two questions that haunt*
*me daily. It would be tedious to write about that, too.*
*Born to be a poet? I wouldn't mind that at all!*
*I miss sending you letters, however. Emailing*
*them feels so wrong. I hope you don't mind*
*But I was thinking about writing and keeping*
*the rest of my work until I can post them*
*to you, again?*

**Of course not, Red! There is no rush, no pressure,**
**and no rules to your art.**
**I enjoy reading your poems and stories in bits and**
**pieces and then witnessing the actual story**
**unfold before my very eyes.**
**I will never regret the day you gave me your**
**journal.**

*I will never regret that day too! Writing to you*
*rescued me from myself*

**I never do much, Red...**
**This was all you!**

*Don't be so modest, Shekinah.*
*You saved me.*

**And how did I do that?**

*You listened.*

*'And when you crush an apple with your teeth, say to it in your heart:*
*"Your seeds shall live in my body,*
*"And the buds of your to-morrow shall blossom in my heart,*
*"And your fragrance shall be my breath,*
*"And together we shall rejoice through all the seasons."'*

—Kahlil Gibran, *The Prophet*

# SPRING
## *The Season of Catharsis*

# GENESIS

Rebirth rises with the dawn.
The fading crescent,
A violent ocean,
Discovered galaxies,
The smouldering sun,
An apocalypse.
My Genesis embraces the end.

# HE GARDENER

"I like touch-me-nots."

"Ah, yes, interesting plants. Ugly, but interesting."

"They are so ugly! But I love them."

"Yes, they look like weeds."

"Magical weeds."

"Do you remember seeing them at the dam when you were a child?"

"No, Dad, I don't remember that all."

"I'm not surprised... when you were a child, I used to take you and your brother for boat rides at the dam. While the other children swam and made sandcastles, you would sit on the banks and play with the touch-me-not. You found them more entertaining than playing with the other kids."

I was genuinely surprised when my father remembered such fine details of my childhood. As I got older, conversations about plants and business ideas never ceased to bore us when we were stuck together. I thought back to the years when I was younger, and he would ignore me and what I thought were brilliant business schemes. I guess it was indoctrinated in him to believe that women were dumb and everything we said was unworthy of a man's time and attention.

If that was how he thought about women, imagine what he thought about a rambling girl. I was frustrated that he never listened to me and angry that he pushed me aside, but paid more attention to my brothers. Over the years, as he aged, he began to talk more. This was normal for both old and quiet people. They get this sudden urge to tell their story because someone needs to hear of all the unjust things they've been through, and my father had the most unjust life of them all. There was no question that this made him rough around the edges.

He was abandoned by both his parents, abused by his uncles, and cheated on by his first wife. He sold fish on the roadside during hot summer days and fought a war in a racist army. His work was bloody, life-threatening and tiring, and when he completed these jobs, he was robbed of all the honest money he earned.

When my grandparents left my dad, they remarried and started new families. Their only son was slowly forgotten in the shadows of their past as they continued with their perfect lives. Sadly, the pattern continued with my father. There was no good example of a man for him to follow. Even the politicians were diabolical men. Both men and women in his life betrayed him, and he became the villain.

*Can you blame him?*

Like the roots of plants, buried deep within the soil, trauma was very much the same. Its roots were anchored within my ancestors and theirs, eventually blooming into the shape of my father.

*How unfair and unjust his life is.*

I hated to admit it, but I could relate more to my father than my mother. He only remembered pure love from his Amma. When I met her, she was a scrawny, strict woman too sick to rise from her bed. She wouldn't tell me sweet stories like my Nani's from my mother's side. Instead, she would inform me of secret recipes that would help me become a strong and healthy Indian woman.

"One teaspoon of castor oil every night would keep your skin free from acne. You see my son's face? No pimples or marks!"

Sometimes, she referred to my father as her son even though he was her grandson. I saw the love in his eyes every time she called him that. It was only through this memory that I realised my father's humanity, and that love was not readily available to him.

In his old age, my father conceived another child with his mistress. I felt no anger or shame towards him as I sat across the table and perceived the wrinkles in his skin and the grey hair that dotted his faded beard. I didn't care that he continued to live *sinfully;* maybe it was because I had forgiven him or because my mother wasn't showing up with busted lips and broken bones anymore. Either way, I was finally content with the mess my parents had created, and I just wanted to talk about plants and gardening with my father before he left for his new family, like his parents did to him.

One day, after a short visit, I watched him approach the gigantic pot at the bottom of our porch stairs. He was unaware of my presence, hidden behind the curtains, as he dug the soil and gradually placed the plant's root in it. He carefully manoeuvred the dirt around the stem, picked up the watering can, and poured its contents on the new plant. The water cascaded slowly like a drizzle. He placed the can down and then tenderly patted the earth. The scene was evidence of a gentleness buried deep within him.

Once satisfied, he left. The gate shut noisily, and his engine revved loudly as he drove away. I pulled the curtains aside, and after a quick struggle with the sliding door, it finally opened. I rushed down the flight of stairs, taking two steps at a time, and stood before the pot. When I recognised the plant, I felt a sudden tug in my chest, where my heart is located.

Droplets ran down the stems and foliage. Its hideous leaves filled the whole pot, but, like poetry, the allure lay within the monstrosity. I swiped the pad of my finger in the middle of the flora's inviting folds and watched as the plant magically closed in on itself. A gale blew in from nowhere, and I pushed back the strands of my hair so I could watch the touch-me-not waltz in the wind.

# EAR TIME

Strangle my delicate throat,
Crack my decorative collarbone,
Rip open my flat-bosomed chest,
Tear the tendons of my heart.
Let the droplets from my window
Fall within your tempo.

Tick-Tock, Tick-Tock.

Then, wash over me like a sudden tide
Take me in your violent current,
Cleanse me from the blood
Your knife drew out within your hours,
The salt of my last swim in you
Burns my gaping wounds.

Tick-Tock, Tick-Tock.

Heal me with your Midas touch,
For gold statues don't feel pain.
Flesh decays within your rhythm.
The reaper, your only ally.
Turn back your hands to my joy
And plummet like dying sparrows.

# A WOMAN'S SPELL

Tossed a penny with a whispered plea,
"Grant me the chance, his chosen one to be."
Down, down the wishing well.
Down, down my damned soul.
For making love a living hell,
Your throne is what I stole.

# NTRODUCTION

I'm not you,
Nor am I them.
*Don't you see?*
I'm simply me.

Lost in your labyrinth,
Striving to mirror you.
But I am me.
The woman I was always meant to be.

I toiled to fit their expectations,
To placate the demons within you,
Yet, I am me.
The woman you loved so carelessly.

Praise Jah for our end,
A death that resurrected me,
Now, here I am,
The woman dancing in all her glory.

I am me.
The woman I was always meant to be,
The woman you loved so carelessly,
The woman dancing in all her glory.

# BROTHER

Life worked out cruelly for us
But its flames did not cremate us.
The world, they walked past us,
Police tape surrounded us,
Only the brave jumped over it,
Rolling straight into our crime scene.
Rebels against the law
Set out to pursue our love.
So, we stand, and we wait,
For the brave-hearted to arrive.
Welcoming them to our bloody scene
With arms wide open, we'll say,
"Come witness our sweet murder. We call it love."

# ROKEN WOMAN

"You are a broken woman!" He roared. The words reverberated until they consumed my soul and branded my life.

For years, all I heard in my mind was, *I am a broken woman.*

Broken and shattered into pieces, I lay on the ground. I was surrounded by feet that once walked beside me.

"Tell me," I pleaded, "Who broke me?"

But I was only answered with the evil cackling of people who I thought loved me.

"Silly girl, it was you who broke yourself."

"Yes, lookie here. Now, this is a whole woman."

An attractive, curvaceous woman was thrust forward in the middle of their vicious circle. I looked up at her, and she looked down at me triumphantly.

"Here is a woman better than you! Look at her." My chin was grabbed by grimy hands and yanked towards the prideful woman, "Broken little things like you must become like her to keep a man. See how she carries herself, brimming with the confidence you never had?"

The woman's tight curls bounced as she giggled delightfully. She basked in their compliments and my torture.

"She is wiser, stronger, emotionally and financially independent. She is more beautiful and whole, and she needs nobody. God favours her like no other. Look at her! Why can't you be like her, you broken, useless woman?" Dirt was kicked into my face as they howled maniacally.

But suddenly, a newfound strength possessed me. I pushed away at the hands that held me captive on the dirty ground. My legs kicked, and a bloody war cry escaped my lips. Men and women dropped heavily, yelling out in pain when the heel of my foot kicked their shins and softer parts of their bodies.

Finally, I rose above them. My legs shook; my knees threatened to give way. Dust clung to my white dress as I stood amidst the chaos. Smoke-like dirt swirled around me. The mob charged back towards me like angry bulls. My fists curled as my scraggy arms recoiled and quickly advanced, bashing into their oncoming faces.

The 'whole woman,' their paragon of perfection, stood apart, trembling. Fear marred her soft features, and it was an ill-fitting mask. She retreated slowly from me like I was the monster. Now, it was my turn to laugh at her.

"You're crazy!" she spat.

"Oh?" I replied coolly and stalked towards her. My eyes were opened wide, and a Cheshire grin was plastered onto my face, "I'm not crazy. No… I'm fucking psychotic!"

Bending low, I scooped a handful of sand and hurled it into her inviting eyes. Her shrill scream halted the mob. Bloodied and bruised, they rushed to console her.

*How simple it was to defeat a beautiful woman.*

When her sobs quieted and her tears washed away the grit, I stood tall before her and her army of idiots.

"Now it's your turn to look at me!" I shrieked, and the sound of my raised voice thrilled me. They glared with hatred, but their attention was on me.

"Yes, I am a broken woman! Like the woman God found at the well with five husbands, I am a broken woman! You may find me at the end of my life with nothing but hope for a better tomorrow. Yes, I am a broken woman!

"You kicked and spat on me while I was already on the ground, yet my faith remains intact. I am a broken woman! You accused me of crimes I couldn't commit alone. The man who was with me was excused from this torture. I am a broken woman! You, holy men and women, judge me, yet I am constantly welcomed to touch the feet of God. Yes, I am a broken woman!

"Look at my flawed shell. No 'whole' woman could endure the same thorns that pierce my skin. My legs tremble. Yet I stand firm. No 'whole' woman could bear the same weight of existence. I embrace the darkness that no 'whole' woman would dare tread. I laugh through my trauma that no 'whole' woman could comprehend. Oh, *whole woman!* God may favour you, and man may admire you. Immortal and mortal.

"But I am a broken woman, eternally loved by both the divine above and the Devil below."

# MOTHER EARTH'S JASMINE

Ivory Corolla cradled in my grandfather's palm
The Gardener plucks her from her creator
Her name, destined for his botanical keep,
My mother meets my father.
Love blossoms before her petals unfold
Separated by bees and butterflies,
Brought together by seasons, unfulfilled,
But forbidden love rots from birth.
A touch, a scream, a generation forged,
Red roses, fruits, weeds, and children
All comes to life in the abandoned garden.
Soil unchanged, yet trauma takes root.
A man, a father, an estranged son,
Sowing and tending a garden anew
While forgotten buds languish in his past,
The Gardener deserts his Eden to decay.
A woman, a nurturer, a beloved sister,
*My Lakshmi,* Amma renames her in death.
Her fragrance, her blistering light lingers,
In Father's verdant memoir and lucid dreams.
She endures drought alongside her offspring,
And Mother Earth blesses the Jasmine
Who forsakes not her own children.

# UNA

The cat distribution system is real,
It's true, you'll see!
I searched for a black cat,
But a black cat found me.
She was fluffy and feisty
(And not too kind).
I took one look at her and thought,
*I should have left this little shit behind.*
My black cat was stubborn
And so very cute!
In a year and a half,
She gave birth to a mute.
She eventually cuddled
After every failed date.
Now I sit back and wonder
What she's up to at Heaven's Gate.
She nibbled and scratched,
Every day I screamed, "Ow!"
But all that pain disappeared
With a simple meow.
"Luna!"
That was her name,
Like the moon, so profound.
I will always remember to this day
That a little black cat and I
Are forever bound.

# THE STARS CHANGE THEIR COURSES

The sound of his laughter, melodious,
His touch, a plunge into a welcoming abyss.
The thought of loss, darker than death herself.
Fallen tears taste sweeter on his parted lips.

Pens that bled on pages now dance delightfully
With his name on the tip of their tongues.
Love resurrects my words, replacing death's sonnets.
With the meeting of our eyes, the multiverse aligns.

In the vast night sky, the stars change their courses,
To gaze upon us.

# FOUR OUT OF THIRTY YEARS

There is a treasure
I hold deep within my spirit
The shadow of you,
Darkening the mistakes of my life.
Until trauma fades, invisible.
My canvas turns black,
Saturated with your colour,
Swallowing the woes of my past.
And on your birthday, in your ears
I would say,
"I have loved you,
Four out of Thirty Years, today"

# MEMORIAL DAY

"I'm getting married!"

If she were alive, I wouldn't announce this. She found the news of relationships mundane, and dating disappointed her. Marital affairs left her unimpressed, and love was just a fleeting feeling in her frail heart.

She would ask me, "Tell me what did you accomplish as a woman in this family?" And I'd be lost for words because, when she was alive, I had no accomplishments. I only sought for love and failed miserably.

If she were alive, I would tell her that her prayers have been answered. That a new generation of women will start with me, and that the curse of man has been broken. If she were alive, I would hold her hand and place my poetry in her soft palm.

"Look at what I did, I wrote about my pain and my mother's and her mother's. I made it art! I'm the first woman in our family to do so. Look at what I did!"

She would respond, teary-eyed, "You told your story. You told *our* story and immortalised us. You made our lives matter; therefore, I, and all your female ancestors, are so proud of you!" She would then bless me, turn salt for me and make me run from the Nazar.

If she were alive, she'd smile brightly when I tell her that I no longer want to die. No, I want to make art, write and be more than a wife or a mother. I want to leave a legacy that is beyond feminine titles. I want to live!

I would tell her this and more, if only my Nani were alive.

# THE DINING ROOM TABLE

I stepped into the lounge, where the granite table stood. It was a polished masterpiece, and its opulence starkly contradicted our poverty. My father crafted it with his own hands, and as I took a seat and traced its edges, a flood of a million memories poured into my mind.

I saw my brother and I sharing bowls of instant noodles for dinner. Laughing, like this act alone could mend what was broken, as we watched anime to erase the morbid reality of our lives. I remembered the sweetness of sugary treats, a feeble balm to soothe the ache of empty bellies.

Recollections of moments filled with dread when voices rose like storms and panic made our little hearts flutter, wild and desperate, like trapped moths. An abused mother until my brother grew strong enough to stop the hand of the abuser. Our teenage years were no kinder, as I recalled our nights of heartache, where we cried and punched walls until our knuckles bled. The feeling of loss was familiar, yet it cut just as deep.

*Nobody loves us.*

Flashbacks of violence replayed. There were bloodied noses, swollen lips, blackened eyes, fractured arms, twisted ankles, and tears. Lots and lots of tears.

Mother slept her days away, and we asked ourselves sarcastically, "What is a father?"

Jokes and sarcasm, that is how we survived our mental turmoil in the asylum we called home.

*Home, sweet home.* The keeper of all the horrid happenings.

I prayed that we would never die in that place, for we wouldn't haunt it but be haunted by it. I pictured our restless ghosts and grinning demons lingering by the beds of a new, unsuspecting family. My brother, ever the prankster, would frighten the children and laugh at their screams as they ran away from his elongated shadow dancing in the dark. The thought made me chuckle, and I snapped out of my grim reverie.

I glanced across the table and saw my mother, red-faced and giggling, her joy unburdened for the first time in years. My brother's wife sat beside him, mid-hysterical laughter, unable to finish the joke that had set her off. Her infectious cackle caused a ripple effect at the table.

Baxter chuckled at the head of the table, and watched his wife with awe as if her snorts were the most beautiful thing he'd ever heard. I choked on my laughter. Tears streamed down my face as I swerved on my seat just in time to catch my fiancé toppling off his chair, convulsed with a hearty guffaw.

Recollections, memories, and nightmares of the past paled in comparison to the scene before me. I gazed at my teary-eyed loved ones, listened to the harmony of their laughter, and realised that everything had changed at the dining room table.

# ANTED

"You're not wanted."
That's alright,
I'm not your criminal.
Tear down your wanted posters,
My shackles are broken.
Prison doors are wide open,

I run as a predator now,
My eyes burn with passion.
After seeing only darkness,
I now see the light.
Screaming,
"Freedom never tasted so sweet!"

# HERNOBYL

Though still paraded as symbols of desire, our bodies are weapons in a perpetual war. To stand naked before a man and witness him unravel into the feeble, trembling creature that he is—is a power that could only be bestowed upon us by a goddess. The harder we fight, the more men rise to challenge, conquer, and murder us emotionally, mentally, spiritually, and physically. There is a constant tug of war on the lifeline of a woman.

*We are Chernobyl.*

Isolated, scorched expanses of radioactive ruin left by the men who once laboured upon us. And, like that forsaken land, they abandon us when we become too volatile and perilous to inhabit. They leave us to rot in the toxic wasteland that they created with their flawed hands. Only for other men to approach and treat us like a ground-breaking discovery, as if our desolation were novel. Although our bodies may be exploited and forgotten like a city ravaged by nuclear fallout, the Earth and her seasons remember.

And while men condemn Chernobyl as barren land, blackened life erupts from her infertile soil. Resilient and unyielding fungi embraces her charred lungs, entwines her broken heart, and rekindles vitality in her ruins.

Spring thrives in Chernobyl's poisoned veins, and so it stirs within the desolate women, too.

*Dear Red,*

*The spring collection utterly enchanted me!*
*Yet, we both understand that real life continues beyond happy endings.*
*I can almost see it now, a pen resting in your hand, sketching the contours of your next story, perhaps for me or perhaps for the world. Who can honestly say?*
*Write and keep on writing, my dearest sister.*
*Write desperately and fervently because, unlike other writers, your life depends on it.*
*And with a yearning that feels like near-starvation, I humbly ask that you share your words with me.*
*Even if they lack poetry, and even when I am gone.*

*Yours truly*
*Shekinah*
*20th December 2024*

**R**ED

## 13th January 2025

*Even when I am gone.*

The queues were endless in every metropolitan service in our country, except at the post office. I was in and out in under ten minutes. I was assured that my parcel would reach Shekinah by the following week.

Over the last seven years, I salvaged every word scribbled in the name of poetry and storytelling. I dug up an old laptop that groaned painfully to life and turned my room inside out in a quest for liberation until, at last, it all came together. Initially, I intended to compile my poems and stories into one tidy document and leave them untouched and unseen. But then, one day, the words refused to be imprisoned.

I was exhilarated, imagining Shekinah's reaction to my debut novella, and I prayed that she wouldn't mind her point of view on the story. It struck me as strange that I hadn't seen her since our first therapy session back when I was a teenager, and moving to another city made it even more difficult for us to meet. Sometimes, I struggled to visualise her, but I brushed it off as one of life's unpredictabilities.

*You never know when you'll see someone for the last time.*

I attempted to envision Shekinah solely through the lens of my imagination. There she was, nestled in the recesses of my mind, older, wiser, and loved throughout the ages, reading the final poem in my book and smiling at its profound implication.

# ED

*27th January 2025*
*In the Beginning...*

*I'm not sure why my father named me Red.*

My fingers danced lightly over the keypad as my next novel began to take shape. Each word emerged, letter by letter, on the glowing screen. There's something purely addictive about words when you become a writer. The power to create worlds, weave universes, and breathe life into beings rests at your fingertips.

*Why did he name me Red?*

If one wishes to feel like God, one should write. Writing is a sacred ritual, an ancient language created by the gods to bear the weight of their existence. Stone tablets, cave walls, and countless parchments carried our histories so we would avoid committing past mistakes. Even in our youth, we carved our names into trees, unwittingly casting old pagan spells upon our generation.

*Names: Red, Baxter, Yasmin, Luna.*

My hand hovered over the keypad. Trauma lived in everything, even in the syllables of a name. Like Jacob, *the deceiver*, we are tethered to the legacy of our names. And those very names are carved into stone in death, keeping us restless beneath the earth.

My father named me Red after a submarine, and when my lover whispers my name, I am reminded of the colour of blood and trauma, the anguish borne by the man who christened me, and how my name feels a misfit against my face.

"Good morning, baby," my fiancé's tender voice scattered all the heavy thoughts of red and trauma.

"Good morning, handsome."

He pressed a comforting kiss on my forehead, glanced at my screen and nodded as if he understood the poetic mess that was written there. This kind, grand gesture made me giggle.

"What's so funny?" he asked, arching his brow in exaggerated curiosity.

"Nothing. I just love you." I beamed up at him, and he grinned in return.

"Before I forget!" He darted out of the room and returned with a box. "You had a package delivered. And, weren't you supposed to be saving money?"

I rolled my eyes dramatically.

"I saw that!" he teased.

"But I didn't order anything, babe. I swear." I frowned, genuinely confused, as I examined the box.

With a loud sigh, he responded lovingly, "Just promise me you'll save your money from now on. I'm off to work. I love you."

"I love you, too!" I hugged him tightly and savoured the embrace before watching him approach his car. He waved until he vanished from my sight down the street. It was our very own little tradition.

*I am in love with a man who loves me.*

I felt the warmth of finally belonging, and as I returned to my desk, I eyed the mysterious package. I was sure I hadn't ordered anything.

*What could it be?*

I grasped the letter opener and carefully sliced through the cardboard. Nothing could have prepared me for what awaited inside. I grabbed my chair and wheeled it towards me haphazardly, plonking down with a sudden dizziness.

Paper cascaded at my feet like snowfall. With trembling hands, I scooped up the sheets, treating each one as if it were made of glass, and placed them reverently on the table. After I emptied the box of its contents, piece by piece, I discarded it and it landed on the floor with a dull thud. Tears threatened to fall when my eyes ran across the organised mess.

Letters. A journal. A book.

*Were these returned to me, or had they never been delivered at all?*

The onset of a panic attack was unmistakable, my skin burned with feverish intensity. Breathing, once an effortless rhythm, became a deliberate, desperate struggle. The air felt too thin, too insubstantial to fill my lungs. Before I succumbed to the spiral into oblivion, I frantically reached for my phone and searched for *her* number, a tether to clarity.

I gasped when I typed her name into the search bar, and the screen stared back, blank and unyielding. I frantically scrolled, typed, and searched but found nothing. No messages, emails or logged calls. Texting, unlike writing, was not magical in any sense, but somehow, her texts disappeared into a void. The pain in my chest intensified and I began to breathe through my mouth, slowly and deeply.

*Writing!*

I bolted towards my bed as soon as the word came to me. Dropping to my knees, I pulled the wooden box from beneath it, flinging the lid aside with urgency. Inside lay the letters, bound tightly with an elastic band. At my desk, I dropped the bundle of letters. With one swift motion, I tore the elastic free, unleashing another avalanche of paper that spilt across the desk.

I held my breath as I unfolded the first letter, and a sob broke from my lips. With desperate urgency, I tore open another, then another, and another.

*Thirteen years.*

Empty, blank pages glared back at me, mocking my sanity. I gasped for air. My eyes raked over the remnants of what had once been beloved treasures. My mind wrestled with this unravelling reality. I ripped the pristine wrapping off the unread book and began to fan myself with the crisp pages. The printed words rouletted and blurred in my periphery, a chaotic dance as the pages fluttered past my eyes.

*Red. My father named me Red. Her father named her-*

Suddenly, her name leapt out at me. I froze, and the book slipped back onto the table. My breath was still ragged as my finger held the page. Of course, I already knew what was written; I was the god of this book. But reading it under the stark light of revelation exposed the truth. With a flick of my finger, the book fell open, revealing her name in all its glory.

*Names. Red. Baxter. Yasmin. Luna.*

But hers was the name that both began and ended my story.

# HEKINAH

To dwell, to settle, to take root,
Grasping the reins of traumata
Divine presence of the Almighty
A feminine energy that abounds
Clouds by day in my Exodus
Fire coruscating in the dead of night,
Honeyed manna from heaven
Writing, my pathos is shaped by you
Breaking boundaries, reaching out
Living amongst your creation
A loving messiah called *her*
Remaining adamant in your role
Benevolent, protector, lover, female.
Gentle ladyfingers on scarred skin,
Nurturing bosoms for all to feed,
Manifestations of the sweet Holy Spirit,
Made visible to a hellion like me.
Were the trinity a woman, it would be you,
And who?
The hidden countenance of God,
An answer to my mother's prayers,
A friend or a sign of impending insanity.
Tell me, is God secreted within your name,
Or is your name God?

# GLOSSARY

**Adam:** The first man God created according to the Bible.

**Agape:** The highest form of unconditional love.

**Alpha:** Used in Christian context to describe God as the beginning.

**Amma:** Tamil for mother or grandmother.

**Baxter:** A boy's name which means baker.

**Ber:** An Indian sweet and sour fruit also known as jujube.

**Beta:** Slang terminology for a passive or weak man.

**Eden:** An earthly paradise in the Bible where God placed Adam and Eve.

**Eve:** The first woman God created according to the Bible.

**Exodus:** Departure (from slavery)/ exit/ journey.

**Gabriel:** An archangel known as the messenger of God.

**Genesis:** The origin or beginning of something.

**Hades:** Hell in Greek mythology.

**Incubus:** A male demon that has sexual intercourse with sleeping women.

**Isa:** Arabic translation of the name Jesus, which means God is salvation.

**Jah:** The personal name of God.

**Josephine:** Female version of the name Joseph, which means God will add or God will increase.

**Lakshmi:** Hindu/ Tamil Goddess of light and prosperity.

**Leviathans:** Large aquatic demons.

**Lucifer:** A Latin name for the devil which translates to morning star.

**Luna:** Latin name meaning moon.

**Manna:** A miraculous edible substance God provided for His people.

**Michael:** An archangel known as the chief or leader of the angels.

**Muthi:** Traditional African medicine or magic. Sometimes, it is used as black magic to harm people.

**Nana:** Urdu for maternal grandfather.

**Nani:** Urdu for maternal grandmother.

**Nazar:** Urdu for bad eyes or evil eyes.

**Omega:** Used in Christian context to describe God as the end.

**Sadiya:** Arabic name meaning lucky or fortunate.

**Satan:** The enemy of God and prince of evil.

**Shekinah:** Shechinah (also known as Shekinah) from the Hebrew "shochen" which means "to dwell," refers to God's indwelling presence and glory—often called "The Divine Presence." It's a feminine word, so we say "She," though it's still the same One God because God isn't confined to a male or female form.

**Thatha:** Tamil for grandfather.

**The Beast:** The Antichrist demon mentioned in Revelations which is the last book of the Bible.

**Yasmin:** Jasmine flower or God's gift.

# UTHOR'S NOTE

In 2024, between July and September, statistical research was conducted in South Africa, and it was with great sadness to find out that although general crime rates dropped in those months, crimes against women and children increased. These crimes were committed in their own homes.

*Three months doesn't seem long, right?*

In this time 43% of the **10 191** rapes reported were women whom their spouses raped. **11 896** women reported being violently assaulted by their domestic partner. **315** children and **957** women were murdered. **1944** children and **14 366** women were assaulted.

These are only the cases reported in *three* months; imagine the cases that were and weren't reported throughout 2024?

With that in mind, abuse and trauma are not normal and should never be normalised. If you have been through any traumatic experience or abuse, I encourage you to seek help **immediately**, whether it's through therapy, a friend or an organisation.

Remember that no woman, man or child is an island. If the facts above, or Red's story, imprinted on your heart, then take it as a sign that you have to do something about it. It is incredibly lonely to suffer from trauma and abuse. So, with the help of a dear friend of mine, Ana Costa, we have provided some helplines. If you or someone you know is a victim of any trauma or abuse, please reach out for help.

# ELPLINES

**Advice Desk for Abused Women**
- Room 1021 A, Durban Magistrates Court
- Contact number: 031 302 4356

**Childline KZN**
- 123 Percy Osborne Road, Berea, Durban
- Contact number: 031 312 0904
- Toll-free number: 116 to speak to a counsellor.
- www.childlinekzn.org.za

**Child Welfare South Africa**
- Contact number: 074 080 8315
- www.childwelfaresa.org.za

**Department of Social Development KZN**
- 24 Bamboo Lane, Pinetown
- Contact number: 031 702 5371
- www.dsd.gov.za

**FAMSA**
- 30 Bulwer Road, Durban
- Contact number: 031 202 8987
- www.famsa.org.za

**Emergency Helplines**
- SAPS Emergency: 10111
- Ambulance/ Fire Brigade: 10177
- Gender-Based Violence Command Centre: 0800 428 428

- STOP Gender Violence: 0800 150 150/ *120*7867#

**Halt Elder Abuse Line (HEAL)**
- Helpline: 0800 003 081

**Human Trafficking Helpline**
- 08000 737 283 (08000 rescues) - 082 455 3664

**People Opposed to Women Abuse (POWA)**
- Contact number: 011 642 4345
- Email: info@powa.co.za

**Substance Abuse Helpline**
- 0800 12 13 14

**TEARS Foundation**
(For victims of domestic violence, sexual assault and child sexual abuse)
- Contact number: 010 590 5920
- Free SMS helpline: *134*7355#
- www.tears.co.za

**The Compassionate Friends**
(Bereavement support and grief counselling)
- 15 KE Masinga Road, North Beach, Durban.
- Contact numbers: 031 266 5847/ 084 332 1876/ 011 440 6322
- Email: tcfsa@mweb.co.za

**The Trauma Centre**
(Trauma counselling and violence prevention services )
- 021 465 7373 / www.trauma.org.za

**The South African Depression and Anxiety Group (SADAG)**

- 24-hour toll-free emergency helplines: 0800 456 789 (mental health helpline) 0800 567 567 (suicide crisis line)
- SMS 32312
- Email: suicideprevent@gmail.com
- Kznsadag@Anxiety.org.za
- www.sadag.org

**Thuthuzela Care Centres**
(Facilities for victims of rape and abuse)

- www.soulcity.org.za

If you are afraid to reach out on your own, feel free to message me on any of the following Instagram accounts for help:

@ARTIST._.SONIA    @RED_SONIA_96    @S.K.YPHOTOGRAPHY

# ACKNOWLEDGMENTS

I am deeply grateful to my mama, Yasmeen Naidoo, for teaching me how to read and write at the age of four. Your love for literature inspired me, and if you ever feel like you failed as a mother, look at this book and know that you didn't.

Thank you to my brother, Kaycé B. Naidoo, for the featured artwork and for walking with me through our trauma. Your strength and integrity taught me to never give up on life. Always remember that you are a man raised by God Himself, and your name is forever written on the palm of His hand.

Thank you to my fiancé, Jaidan Jairaj, for listening to me read every poem and short story in this book. I'm so sorry for traumatising you! Thank you for loving me and pushing me to follow my dreams. I don't write sad poems anymore because of you.

Thank you to my dad, Butler V. Naidoo, for teaching me to be strong, ambitious, independent and, oh, so very angry with the world. *I am my father's daughter.*

Thank you to my best friend, Lavasha Naidoo, for the review, wine sessions, *hooga* nights and your friendship. To Shanai C. Naidoo, for the seven years of hearing me say, "I'm going to write a book!" and believing me. And to my siblings, Christina T. Naidoo and Blake E. Naidoo, for your love and encouragement.

To my in-laws, Carol, Rakesh, Sharia Jairaj, and their extended family—thank you for supporting my writing journey. Uncle Collin Pillay, thank you for constantly reminding me not to allow your nephew (my fiancé) to distract me from finishing my novella. And to Nazneen Haneef, thank you for letting me flood your inbox!

To Sister Muggins, Pastor Darin and the ladies in our Tuesday morning meeting—here and in heaven—thank you for your prayers. God has answered them!

To Ekta Somera and Sana-Bella Ebrahim, thank you for your reviews. To Alta H. Haffner, thank you for bringing this book to life. To Pragashnie Naidoo and Glynus Horning, thank you for your thoughtful editing and review. And to Ana Costa for advising me to use the helplines in our esteemed anthology, *320 Days of Sunshine*.

A big, warm thank you to author Arini Vlotman. It was fate that led me to you, which led me to Sakura Book Publishing. And to James N. McManus for the beautiful review and foreword.

Lastly, I thank God for all the trauma and the art it inspired.

# ABOUT THE AUTHOR

Born and raised in Durban, South Africa, **Sonia Naidoo** is a multi-talented poet, author, ghostwriter, photographer and artist. She is engaged to Jaidan Jairaj, a South African actor and businessman, and she is a proud mum of eight cats.

Her passion for literature blossomed at the tender age of four, nurtured by her mother, Yasmeen Naidoo, who taught her to read and write. Sonia's writing journey began at the age of fifteen, when she and her best friend, Lavasha Naidoo, started crafting short fanfiction stories inspired by their favourite books and movies. During this time, she also turned to poetry to navigate the challenges of anxiety and depression.

Sonia holds a Higher Certificate in Photography, a Certificate in Business Administration, and Diplomas in Biblical Studies as well as English Language and Literature. She also runs a freelance photography business named *S K Y-Photography.*

*Traumata, The Seasons of Femininity,* is her debut novella.

# REFERENCES

**Author's note:**

- https://www.da.org.za/2024/11/crime-stats-reveal-shocking-violence-against-women-and-children
- *320 Days of Sunshine, Memoirs & Stories from KwaZulu-Natal,* edited by AC Costa and illustrated by Carmen Gee

**Glossary:**

- https://www.chabad.org/library/article_cdo/aid/2438527/jewish/The-Shechina.htm#:~:text=The%20Freeman%20Files-,G%E2%80%91d%20as%20She,us%20and%20return%20to%20one.

Quotes:

- The Prophet by Kahlil Gibran (1991 edition published by Mandarin Paperbacks)

www.ingramcontent.com/pod-product-compliance
Lightning Source LLC
Chambersburg PA
CBHW061524020726
47502CB00006B/2228